ALSO BY DAWN McNIFF

Little Celeste

Worry Magic

Dawn McNiff

HOT
KEY
BOOKS

First published in Great Britain in 2015 by Hot Key Books
Northburgh House, 10 Northburgh Street, London EC1V 0AT

A CIP catalogue record for this book is available from the British Library.

ISBN: 978-1-4714-0371-2

1

This book is typeset in 11pt Sabon using Atomik ePublisher

Printed and bound by Clays Ltd, St Ives Plc

www.hotkeybooks.com

Hot Key Books is part of the Bonnier Publishing Group
www.bonnierpublishing.com

FOR TUFTA, PLUD AND PIGOTHY xx

Chapter One

There was a pig in our lounge.

It was kind of the last straw, really. What with poor Gran so bad in hospital, and Dad in his worst mood ever.

What *was* Mum thinking?

I knelt down on the carpet and watched the pig oink around the room like a loon. OK, he was only small – so small he could sit in my hands. And he *was* very cute. But he was still a blinking pig.

INSIDE OUR HOUSE.

Of course it wasn't exactly a surprise. Mum had always brought back animals from the sanctuary. She'd volunteered there for my whole, entire life, so for as long as I could remember, we'd had bald hamsters, ducks with broken wings, rabbits with poorly tummies, mumless kittens – basically any ones that needed extra-special love. Some got new homes and some stayed, but Mum could never resist a sad, furry face. We'd even had a lame pony on the back lawn once.

But she was pushing her luck with this pig . . .

Because Dad was going to FLIP out. Like, *totally* shout his head off.

Had she forgotten that argument the other night? Dad'd yelled that we couldn't afford any new pets, not even a caterpillar. Then he'd stormed off, but not to sulk in his precious Shed in the garden like usual. He went out to town or somewhere, and didn't get in until past midnight – and Dad *never* stayed out late.

I sighed. I just knew we were heading for the biggest load of pig-shaped trouble EVER.

I wanted to try and talk Mum out of it, but I couldn't even get a word in edgeways – she was yacking on at me at a million miles an hour. So I just sat there staring at the pig, chewing my lip and waiting for a gap.

'Of course he won't get much bigger when he grows up, because he's one of those micro-pigs. You know . . . the girl off that breakfast show's got one – Kelly What's-her-face with the nice hair . . .' she was gabbling.

I'd seen micro-pigs on the telly too. Some scientist had invented them for dumb-head celebrities to keep as handbag pets – poor little things.

'And can you BELIEVE someone abandoned him?' she rattled on. 'No one at the sanctuary can understand it because micro-pigs can be expensive to buy. And he's so schweeeeet too, aren't yooooou . . .' She picked the piglet up and kissed him right on his weeny snout while he squirmed.

She searched me for a smile. 'Oh come on, don't you think he is a tiny bit gorgeous, Courtney?'

'Well, yeah, 'course, Mum,' I said. 'But what about . . .'

'Shall we call him Widget?' she said, talking right over me. 'I think that suits him, don't you?' She gazed at the piglet, her eyes shining like she was loved up, and my heart sank even more. Now she'd named him too. I could tell she had a sly, secret plan to keep him forever.

I glanced at the clock . . . 4.35 p.m. already. I hugged my knees as more and more worry snaked around in my tummy. Dad was working all hours at the mo, trying to get his new gardening business off the ground – but even he couldn't work in the dark. I reckoned he wouldn't be long – maybe an hour, tops.

I did an extra-big sigh and rubbed my face hard with my palms . . . and then Mum *finally* caught my look. She stopped nattering for half a second.

'I'm only fostering him, of course,' she said, glancing away shiftily. 'Really, Courts, he won't stay long – just while he needs bottle-feeding. Even Dad can understand that . . . and anyway, it's not just up to *him*!'

I shook my head. Nope, Dad definitely wouldn't understand! He'd say Mum was supposed to be finding a new job rather than messing about with dopey pigs. I knew she HAD applied for some jobs, but she never seemed to get them – probably cos the sanctuary had to come first.

'No, really, Mum, Dad won't . . . !' I began.

'Oh, look, he wants a nice cuddle from his big sis,' she said. She handed me the tiny piglet like he was her newborn baba. He lay wriggling in my arms with his little trotters in the air, looking up at me with his funny, babyish snouty face. It was true – he really was the sweetest thing, but . . . BIG but!

'Aww – see? Adorable, isn't he?' Mum said, taking the piglet off me. 'It's really *impossible* not to like him.' She turned and called to my big brother, who was still in his school uniform and superglued to his laptop in the corner. 'YOU like him, don't you, Kylsie?'

'Er . . . yeah, whatever, Mum,' said Kyle, without even looking over.

Great. Utterly useless as usual. Kyle only cared

about stuff like football, computers and being brainy. He was never any help at all.

And Widget wasn't exactly helping either. He snuffled around, and then did a very un-cute poo right next to where I was sitting on the carpet.

Ewww! I jumped to my feet.

'Whoopsie, babycake!' cooed Mum, scooping him up. 'I'll clean that up in a minute, but now it's time for your tea.' And she bustled out with the tiny pig cradled in her arms, totally missing my OMG-this-can't-be-happening face.

I stepped over the poo, and crashed down onto the sofa. And then leapt straight up with a big OWWW. I chucked a dirty plate, fork and a pair of football boots on the floor and sat down again. This place was rotting without Gran around. It was literally turning to poo. Pig poo.

Gran lived next door, just the other side of the wall, but she was always round ours, tidying and just being nice. Or used to be. Until she had to go to hospital the other week. Me and Kyle hadn't even got to visit her yet, because Dad said she was just too ill, with loads of horrid tubes in her and stuff – shudder.

It was so horrible. Poor Gran . . .

'Of course, Dad's going to hit the roof,' Kyle said, still not looking away from his screen. 'You know . . . about the pig.'

Duh, of course he was!

My brother was a great one for saying obvious things like that. He always said them in a voice like they were just interesting facts. Kyle liked facts a lot.

'So . . . I'd go out in a minute if I were you,' he said quietly, with his eyes still on his screen. 'I am.'

'Out? No! We gotta do something about this before Dad gets back.' I tutted.

Kyle just rolled his eyes under his glasses, and shook his head.

I made a face at him. It was just like Kyle. He always disappeared – poof! – whenever Mum and Dad kicked off. But I knew if I went out I'd just worry myself half sick about what was happening at home. No, I had to at least TRY and stop this fight . . .

All I needed was a Brilliant Plan . . .

I pulled up my hood, my brain on full speed . . .
So should I steal Widget and hide him? But where?
And Mum'd never let her darling babykins out
of her sight, would she, so . . . er . . . what else?

I started gnawing at my nails. I had that
disgusting 'stop-biting' stuff painted on them,
but it never worked when I got really worried. I
didn't even notice the yucky bitter taste.

Gran's cat, Pudding, came stalking into the
room just then. He was living round ours at the
moment, while Gran wasn't at home.

Puddy was the best cat ever. Mum had got him
from the sanctuary, and Gran'd adopted him. He
was black with a white tummy, face and paws
like he'd fallen in some melted marshmallow, and
he was always super-purry and cuddly. The only
problem was keeping him away from Henners'
cage. Henners – short for Henry the Eighth – was
Dad's fat, white rat. He came from the sanctuary
too, and Mum'd tried to make him like her best,
but Henners only loved Dad. And Dad loved-
loved-*loved* Henners back – more than his own

children, more than Brighton FC, more than basically his own life. If Puddy got Henners, the world would explode with a big kaboom.

Puddy sniffed the piglet poo, and backed away, hissing around the room, and then leapt on my lap. He curled up, padding and needling my knees with his claws and purring loudly. I buried my face in his fur, tickling him under his chubby little chin. Pudds was on my side, at least. And he smelt lovely too – a bit like Gran's house . . . washing powder and fairy cakes.

'Oh Puddy-cat, we miss Gran too much, don't we?' I whispered to him. 'If Gran was here, she'd know what to do about all this piglet trouble.'

I sighed.

Well, I supposed I could start by tidying up . . . like Gran always did. Dad hated mess – he even kept his veg patch super-neat – so it wouldn't help if the house looked so grotty.

But I wasn't doing the pig poo – Mum could do THAT!

Pudds was kipping on me, twitching in his sleep and purring like he was dreaming happy, kittenish dreams. I slid him off my lap onto a cushion, got up and began bundling things behind the sofa. I could sort it all out later.

But I was just finishing straightening the cushions how Dad liked them, when the front door banged.

A loud, grumpy bang.

A Dad-ish kind of bang.

I froze.

'Dad's back,' said Obvious Fact Man in the corner. 'He's early.'

'Yes, I've got ears too!' I mouthed, glaring round at him.

My breathing sped up and I started gulping. I wanted to run for Widget and stuff him up my jumper – anything to stop Dad seeing him. But I could already hear the porch door sliding open . . .

In the distance I was sure I could hear oinking.

'No, Widget . . . shhhh!' I said under my breath, my tummy rolling over and over with panic.

Dad was going to take one look at Widget and do his nut. Then he might huff off and stay out late again.

Or maybe he might actually leave forever – like Maisie Gable's dad did in the summer.

Then I wouldn't have Gran.

Or Dad . . .

Oh, everything was going so wrong . . .

Suddenly I felt so spinny I had to hold onto the sofa arm.

I caught my breath, and my face went hot.

Whoa . . . weird . . . what was *happening* to me?

Chapter Two

Dad thumped past the lounge door in his socks.

Towards the kitchen.

Where Mum and Widget were.

I ran to the lounge door, flapping my arms about, not knowing what to do, my heart galloping.

But it was too late.

I peered round the corner into the hall, just as Widget gave an extra loud, sharp squeal.

Dad jumped at the noise, and froze in the kitchen doorway.

Then he shook his head and pointed into the kitchen.

'Donna – tell me that isn't a *pig* behind the washing machine,' he said in a tired voice. 'Tell me my eyes are playing tricks on me.'

'It's a micro-piglet actually,' Mum said, a bit grumpily. 'And they're *supposed* to live indoors as pets . . .'

'God help me – isn't this house in enough of a mess?!' Dad snapped back. 'But no – now you're turning it into an actual PIG STY!'

'Oh, don't start, Andy!' Mum huffed. 'And he's only here for a bit, so I can hand-feed him . . .'

'Huh, yeah, how many times have I heard *that* one?!' Dad's voice had gone really hard and cold. 'Absolutely no way . . . he has to go RIGHT NOW.'

'Well, tough luck, because I say he's *staying*!' said Mum, her voice going all high and squeaky.

Oh no, I just KNEW this was going to happen – they were cooking up a big fight again. A wave of heat rushed up me. I was trying to breathe slower, but I couldn't. I whirled around at Kyle, making desperate faces at him.

'Leave it, Courts,' he said, his eyes flicking off his screen for a millisecond. 'Just keep well out.'

Great. No use at all AGAIN.

I made a face at him and went out into the hall on wobbly legs. Ooh, why was I feeling so faint and weird?

Mum and Dad's voices were getting louder – they were revving up and up.

I stood in the kitchen doorway, but they didn't even seem to notice me.

'HOW can you be so mean?' Mum was shrieking. 'Poor little orphan piglet needs TLC and a few drops of milk, and you won't . . .'

'For pity's sake, Donna! We're not a flipping animal hospital!' Dad was bright red and his eyes were bulging out. 'We've been through this already . . . We have debts. We CANNOT afford any new animals! GET IT?'

'Mum . . . Dad!' I began.

But I got drowned out as Mum blew up at Dad again:

'Oh, hark at the big BOSS man. Well, I live here too! I get a say, you know . . .' She was totally off on onc.

But I stopped listening for a moment. Because I'd suddenly noticed a ham quiche, out on the side, ready for tea. Ugh, no . . . Dad hated quiche – he said it looked like cold sick in a pastry case, and Mum knew that. I hoped he didn't spot it – the mood he was in right now, he might karate-chop it.

Dad was shaking his head over and over again as Mum went on and on. He was frowning so much that his bald head had wrinkled up into big ridges.

Then he put his hand up to stop her. 'Hey, wait, here's an idea for you, Donna. Why don't you try harder to get a job instead of thinking of ways to spend? You know, like *grown-ups* do . . .'

Ooh, he was having a right old dig.

Mum roared, nearly lifting off the ground. Her frizzy hair boinged as she waved her arms about, yelling stuff.

This got Widget so excited that he started running races round and round their feet, squealing and waggling his curly tail.

Dad glared down at him, and threw up his arms.

'Right, STOP! I'm not listening to any more!' he bellowed over the din. 'I've really had it!' he hissed.

Oh dear . . . oh no, that didn't sound good! My head came over so swimmy I had to hold onto the door handle.

Dad turned to walk out of the kitchen and sort of jumped, like he was surprised to see me there. But then he just squeezed past me, muttering and swearing.

I got out of the way as Mum rushed past me too, shouting-shouting-shouting in one big whoosh of crossness at Dad's back.

Dad blanked her, stamping his feet back into his trainers.

What? Was he going out already? But he'd only just got in . . . My heart flipped over. Why couldn't he just go and hide in his Shed, or tidy leaves off his veg patch, if he wanted to get away from Mum?

My dizzy feeling was getting worse . . . and worse.

'Dad – where're yo-o-u going . . . ?' My voice sounded far away in my ears. 'Da-a-d . . . ?'

My head dipped and spun. I caught hold of the radiator to try and get steady, but the world was whirling.

And then the weird thing happened.

Suddenly I couldn't keep my eyes open for a second longer. My legs crumpled under me, and I slid down the wall in an odd, SLO-O-OW sort of faint.

Onto the floor.

Conked out asleep.

Completely sparko.

Chapter Three

I really was asleep cos I had this odd kind of dream – all these broken-up pictures that skidded away from me when I tried to look at them properly.

Dad taking his shoes off. Mum and Dad like dark silhouettes, heads together, talking softly. Mum in her green coat carrying Widget. Dad holding something with red and yellow flapping pages. Sweetcorn . . . slices of pepperoni . . .

And then suddenly the pictures just faded away like the end of a film.

I opened my eyes, blinking. I was still lying on the hall rug.

I looked up and Mum was peering down at me, her face white, her eyes starey. Kyle was standing right behind her, peering over her shoulder at me, his glasses pushed up on his head.

Dad was crouching down next to me.

'Spud?' said Dad softly, stroking my hair out of my face. He hadn't called me Spud for a very long time – it was his nickname for me when I was tiny. 'You OK?'

'Yeah, yeah, Dad.' I nodded. Although actually I had NO idea what'd just happened to me.

I went to sit up.

'No, just stay still for a minute, darling,' Mum said. She leant over Dad and put a cool hand on my forehead, her faced all pinched.

'Really, I'm OK, Mum,' I said.

Dad nodded up at Mum. 'She's fine, Donna.' But he said it in a nice voice for once – sort of gentle. 'I think she just fainted.'

Did I faint? No, I was sure I'd been *asleep* . . .
but since when did I fall asleep in the middle of
the flipping day?

'Come on – hup you come now.' Dad scooped
me up into his arms like I was a baby again, and
carried me to the sofa. Mum followed behind,
putting cushions under my head, and covering
me up with her knitted throw. I saw Kyle hover
in the doorway for a minute, and then slip away
up the stairs.

Mum and Dad stood in the middle of the
lounge, half whispering. I tried to catch their
words, looking back and forth between them.

'Maybe she has a bug?'

'No, she hasn't got a fever – I felt her
forehead . . .'

'So what was it? Like a panic attack . . . ?'

Dad glanced down at me and saw my ears
wagging. He tugged Mum's arm and they went
right through into the hall where I couldn't hear,
but I could still see them

They were stood close together. Two shadows
against the street-lit glass porch door.

And that was when my dream suddenly filled my head again.

Silhouettes! This was exactly what I'd seen. Dark shapes . . .

Then I watched Dad kick off his trainers, still talking nicely with Mum. Uh . . . ? But that was like my dream too!

I rubbed my eyes. This was all a bit weird.

And then it just kept getting weirder and weirder.

Mum came back in, and put her hand on my head again.

'How you feeling now?

I nodded. 'I'm *honestly* fine.' And I really was.

'OK . . .' she said, doubtfully. 'You know, I think you were right – it *would* be better if I took Widget back.' But she whispered it, like the words hurt her to say.

Really? Oh phew!

'Karen's on duty at the sanctuary tonight, so she can take him home with her,' Mum said, picking up Widget.

I nodded slowly, but my brain was doing cartwheels.

Mum leaving with Widget . . . just like in my dream.

'Is that OK, darling?' Mum said, giving me a long look and pulling on her green coat. 'Dad's going to sort tea . . . I'll be back in a bit.'

Her GREEN coat . . . That was in my dream too.

What was going ON?

I nodded again, trying to look normal.

But when Mum hurried out, I just lay there gawping, listening to Widget squeak in the hall, and the front door clunk as Mum left with him.

Was I losing it, or *what*? Dreams don't just come true!

Dad was scrabbling about in the sideboard drawer. And when he turned round, I nearly rolled off the sofa. He flapped some red and yellow pages at me.

A takeaway menu . . .

He pointed at it, and I knew what he was going to say even before he'd opened his mouth.

'Sweetcorn and pepperoni – your favourite, madame?'

OMG.

We never had takeaway these days – way too expensive.

And OMG times a million OMGs – that was the final piece of my dream.

Now the whole thing had all come ABSOLUTELY TRUE! Every teeny-tiny bit of it.

Whoa! An amazing thought fizzled right through me . . .

This was like actual MAGIC . . .

Magic that had cast a spell on Mum and Dad and brainwashed them into being nicer. Magic that had sorted out everything I'd been panicking about . . . Widget, and even the dumb quiche-for-tea.

Like a special kind of magic that fixed worrying things . . .

Worry magic.

But, pah, noooo, I was going loony . . . I loved magic stuff – me and my best friend Lois knew all the Harry Potter books off by heart – but this was proper cuckoo. Only people in storybooks had *magic* powers. Not real, alive people like me.

I fell back on my cushion and listened to Dad ordering the pizzas out in the hall, tingling all over.

But – wow – if this was really and truly happening, it was just too EPIC.

Chapter Four

We all sat in front of the TV later and ate the pizza together, which hardly ever happened any more. Dad often had his tea in his Shed if it wasn't too freezing, especially since he'd got a better radio and comfier chair in there. It was like his den.

I sat right in the middle of Mum and Dad on the sofa, and Kyle was slumped over the armchair. No one spoke much, but at least no one was yelling. And anyway all I could do was chomp on my pizza and stare at the telly in a daze. I was still feeling so weirded out by all that dream stuff.

When we'd finished, Mum went off to do things in the kitchen, and Dad changed the channel to some boring darts match.

Kyle just sat there, chewing his pen and frowning at one of his duh-brained sudoku puzzles. But when Dad went out to the loo, Kyle started looking at me a bit funny and sideways. He sighed, and I thought he was going to say something – but then he just stuffed some leftover pizza crusts from the box into his mouth instead.

'Eww, those weren't even your crusts,' I said.

He made one of his cross-eyed monster faces at me, and ate with his mouth really wide open, so I could see all his chewed-up pizza.

'You are SO gross,' I said.

Dad came back in just at that minute.

'Kyle – leave it out, will you!' he snapped, screwing up his nose as he sat back down.

Kyle didn't say anything – he just glared at his puzzle, his face suddenly all dark and grim. Then he got up, grabbed his laptop, and stalked out of the room and up the stairs two at a time.

Grumpeeee!

I looked at Dad, but luckily he didn't seem to have noticed. His eyes were stuck back on the darts.

What had got into Kyle? I felt some worry prickle in my tummy again. Why did he have to be so stupidly moody? If I really had magicked things calmer, he'd better not go and ruin it . . .

But actually the house went lovely and chilled out after that.

Mum was still in the kitchen, Dad went off to have his bath, and I was left by myself in the lounge. I turned the telly to silent – ahhhh! It was so quiet . . .

There was a funny noise outside the window . . . but it was just Puddy, standing up on his back paws, scratching on the glass – *chut-chut-chut* – to come in. He was *always* doing that. I let him in and he cuddled up in a ball against my tummy, like a hot-water bottle.

Then I listened to his loud, sleepy purr, and let my mind rewind and replay my magic dream and all its coming-trueness over and over again – until everything started blurring together, and it felt like the whole thing might've been one big dream.

Had it *really* happened?

I just couldn't get my head round it.

I stretched and yawned.

Still, I wasn't complaining.

Magic or no magic, everything was calm now.

Chapter Five

I was still lazing on the sofa when Dad plodded back downstairs and popped his head round the door. He looked all scrubbed in his dressing gown, and was wafting a lemon-soap smell. He gave me a hard look like he was checking up on me. Then he did a thumbs-up, and padded off towards the kitchen to get his usual after-bath cuppa.

But then one second later, there was a loud clink and a smash, and –

'ARGGGGGH! What THE . . . !'

I nearly jumped out of my skin. Puddy bounced in the air and shot out the door.

Dad's voice boomed in the kitchen –

'ARRGH! Who left that on the floor?' he yelled.

What was going on?

I legged it to the kitchen and stopped dead in the doorway.

Dad was standing in a puddle of white, gooey stuff, next to a broken, upside-down dish. And it looked like he'd trodden on the edge of the dish and flipped it over, because loads of the goo had flicked up his legs and dressing gown, and all over one of the cupboards. There were even some small dollops on the window.

Mum was just leaning against the side, giggling helplessly. Her shoulders were shaking like mad, and she'd gone bright pink.

'Oh yeah, ha, ha!' Dad said, although he didn't sound *too* angry. 'What IS it?' He tried to flick some splodge off his leg, but it was all stuck to his hairs.

'B-b-baby rice,' spluttered Mum through her giggles, wiping away a tear. 'I put it down for the p-p-piglet, but he didn't like it.'

Dad did a big sigh, but he caught my eye, and for a tiny moment, I thought I saw the corner of his mouth twitch. I stared at him hard, not knowing whether to smile, hoping he might be catching Mum's giggles. Please, Dad – just laugh! It's just some silly, spilt piglet rice.

'Blinking madhouse,' he muttered. 'I'm gonna need a clean sponge.' And he tugged open a cupboard.

But then he stopped completely still, his face clouding over as he glared into the cupboard. He pressed his lips hard together, squashing my hopes of a smile. And then without a word he took some things out and lined them up neatly on the working surface next to Mum.

Baby wipes. Two boxes of baby rice. A packet of rusks. A big tin of powdered baby milk. A new feeding bottle with teddies on . . .

'I wasn't aware we had a baby,' he said in a tight voice.

I felt myself stiffen. Uh oh . . . look out! I started gulping. If the magic really *had* made Dad nicer earlier on, then it looked like it had worn off already. Because OMG, he was giving Mum daggers now.

'Those are just a few bits I got for the piglet,' Mum said, her giggles vanishing. 'I'll take it all to the sanctuary for him tomorrow.'

'Ah right, I see,' Dad snapped. 'And I s'pose you bought it all with the *thin air* in our bank account, did you?' His ears had gone pink and were wriggling up and down as he spoke. '*Organic* milk too. Only the best, eh!'

Mum scowled then, and my heart did a blip. Oh no, they were going off on one again – I could just tell by their faces . . .

How could I get them apart? What could I do?!

'Andy, will you just GET OFF my case for once?' Mum snapped, folding her arms hard across her chest.

'On your case? What case is that, then? A nutcase? A hopeless case . . .' Dad was being well sarky. Mum hated it when he got like that.

My heart started beating fast in my throat, and my eyes went blurry.

Oh, why did they keep arguing so much? They never stopped – and it was getting worse and worse. I just wished Gran was here – sometimes she could referee when they got like this. Because they wouldn't listen to me. They seemed to have forgotten I was even there.

I blinked hard and gulped down some breaths.

'And this flipping stuff is gluing me to the floor!' growled Dad, lifting one leg, his slipper squelching off the lino.

'Well, perhaps next time you'll look where you put your big feet!' Mum said, swinging away to the sink. 'In the meantime, get mopping!'

'WHAT?' spluttered Dad. 'I'm not cleaning this up . . . you left the dish there.'

Oh . . . my head was muggy . . . heavy . . .

My throat was so tight I felt like I couldn't get enough air.

I sat down with a bump on the kitchen stool. I held my head in my hands to try and stop it from wobbling. But it was no good. My eyelids were closing.

I fell forward onto all fours . . .

'Courtney . . . ?' I could hear Mum's voice . . . somewhere . . . echoing in my brain . . .

And then I just face-planted into the rice gloop on the floor.

I was gone.

Fast asleep again.

Chapter Six

I knew I was dreaming this time – while it was actually happening. But it wasn't a proper dream again – just lots of little glimpses of random things . . .

Mum with a pink mop, Dad standing on a stool. Both of them smiling. The *'You've Been Framed!'* theme tune . . .

And then a fade to nothing.

Well, that was weird. What was *that* all about?

I felt myself lift off the floor, and my eyes flew open. Dad was picking me up and sort of staggering.

He sat down heavily on the big kitchen chair and he held me on his lap. He was hugging me so tight that my face was getting squashed against his fluffy dressing gown, which was all damp and smelt of lemon sweets. I pushed away from him, and sat bolt upright, blinking.

Mum knelt down next to me.

'Courts?' she said, her voice all quivery. 'You OK?' She was squeezing my leg hard, like she was checking I was in there.

'Ow! Yes, yes, Mum . . . I'm fine.'

Kyle came clumping in just then, holding an empty mug. He stopped in the doorway.

'What's going on *now*?' he asked.

I slid off Dad's lap, and shook myself.

'Nothing,' I said. But actually I was hoping that a LOT of magic had been going on.

I looked around at everyone. Had the dream done its business again?

Really? Had it?!

Kyle shrugged and turned away, pulling the instant hot choc jar out of the cupboard. I swear he lived off that stuff.

'No, no, Courts – please sit down. I really think you should rest a bit,' said Mum.

Mum and Dad were signalling to each other.

'Yes, sit while I get you a drink,' agreed Dad, getting up and patting the chair cushion. 'Actually, Kyle, make your sister a hot choc too, will you?'

'Yes *sir*,' muttered Kyle under his breath, so Dad didn't hear. He looked really hacked off, but he got another mug out.

He handed me my hot choc without looking at me, and then shuffled out.

And so I sat there, sipping away, with about ten cushions stuffed behind me like I was on a throne, while Mum and Dad cleaned the kitchen.

Together.

Really.

They were both doing it, and no one was even moaning.

Mum and Dad were being nice to each other again. And it could only be for one reason . . .

THE WORRY MAGIC HAD WORKED!

And when I saw Mum tug the pink mop out of the cupboard I was even more sure.

Aha! It was like watching a repeat on telly that you'd already seen. I kept knowing what would happen next.

While Mum mopped, Dad stood on the stool and wiped the rice blobs off the window, his hairy-man legs sticking out beneath his dressing gown. TICK! Just like in my dream.

And THEN even more amazing . . . Dad turned the kitchen telly on, and . . . I held my breath . . . would it be?

And it was. TICK! The '*You've Been Framed!*' theme tune blared out.

Just wow. Gigantic, huge, massive WOW.

I was so blown away, I had to hide my stunned face behind my mug.

Yep, there was no doubt this time. It had happened twice now. This was magic. Proper, REAL magic!

Dad stopped wiping the cupboards to watch a man go flying head-first into a snowdrift. He giggled and winked at me, and then Mum smiled too. A tired, tight smile. But she actually *smiled* at Dad.

That just never happened these days . . .

By now the kitchen was spotless, and Mum started shooing me upstairs to have a bath.

'Early night for you,' she said. As I got to my feet, she grabbed me and hugged my head. 'And, darling – just so you know – me and Dad both think you should go to the doctor's tomorrow. Just for a little check-up – you know, to see why you fainted,' she said, twirling a long strand of my hair. 'That OK?'

I thought about saying that I hadn't fainted, but I'd actually fallen asleep and dreamt everything better in a *magic* sort of way. But obviously I knew they'd never believe me, and I'd sound weird. And Dad was nodding, agreeing with Mum for once, so I just shrugged and nodded too, and went upstairs.

As I passed Kyle's room, I saw him hunched over his laptop in the dark apart from a pool of light from his desk lamp.

I stopped by his door for a second. I knew it was a dumb idea, but I suddenly really, *really* wanted to tell him about my magic.

But no . . . there was no point – he'd just laugh in my face. Kyle liked real things you could kick with a football boot or look up on Google. Magic was deffo NOT his bag.

I walked on past to the bathroom and turned on the bath taps full blast.

Kyle was a boring old muggle-face, but maybe I could tell Lois. Lois had been my best friend since Year Two, and our favourite game when we were smaller was Being At Hogwarts and Making Up Spells. But somehow now it turned out that I really *was* a bit magic.

Ha, ha.

I poured loads of peach bubble bath into the water, and whipped up masses of sweet foam.

Yes, I was going tell Lois. The next day at school.

I couldn't wait . . .

I stepped into the deep bath and sank right down into it, floating off the bottom and blowing at the crackly bubbles.

Now something else was fizzling through my brain.

Exciting, but super-scary.

If the worry magic could fix things, could it even make GRAN better?

COULD IT?

And what if I worried about Gran actually *on purpose?* Could I panic myself, bring on the magic, and CURE her?

Whoa! This was so freaky.

But it was worth a try . . . and why not RIGHT NOW?

I ducked right under the water, and screwed up my eyes tight. I didn't really want to, but I made myself think about all the horrible, scary stuff to do with Gran . . .

Coming home that day to find her gone . . . Dad telling us about the ambulance . . . his frightened face . . .

I imagined Gran lying there with her tubes stuck in her . . . not getting better . . .

Brrrrrrrr!

I shivered under the water, and popped my head out with a gasp, my heart beating loudly in my ears. Ugh, it was working. I was really upsetting myself. But I couldn't have a worry-dream in the bath – I might drown.

I clambered out, wrapped myself up in a huge towel, sat on the bathroom floor, and carried on worrying and worrying.

I worried until tears were dripping off my cheeks.

But still no dizzy feeling came.

Still no magic . . .

I sighed, and rubbed my face hard with my towel.

It was hopeless. I couldn't MAKE myself conk out or have a dream. It was like trying to sneeze – just impossible.

The magic didn't seem to work long-distance. But I was sure that if I saw poor, ill Gran – up close, with my own eyes – I'd get so, so, SO worried that the magic would come straight away.

I pulled my dressing gown off the back of the door, and dragged it on.

Dad had promised to take me to the hospital on Saturday, if Gran was well enough.

That was the day after tomorrow.

Yes . . .

Please come then, worry magic!

Chapter Seven

At breakfast, Mum told me she'd got me a doctor's appointment at ten to four that afternoon, She um-ed and ahh-ed, but eventually she said I could go to school and meet her at the doc's after home-time – but if I felt faint in the day, even a bit, I should tell a teacher straight away.

Yeah, yeah, Mum – like I was going to tell a teacher . . . All I could think about was getting to school and telling LOIS about the magic. I felt like if I didn't tell her soon, I'd go pop.

But when I got there, school was really annoying.

I hardly saw Lois all day, and never by herself. Now we were at secondary we had lots of different lessons and only English, Art and registration together. And I knew I couldn't wait for her after school cos I had to rush off to meet Mum at the doc's.

But then when I pushed through the corridor to the lockers after last lesson, I was amazed to find Lois already there, out on time for once. She bear-hugged me, her long plait swinging in my face.

'Hey, it's not raining – shall we go up the park for a bit?' she said. 'We could buy some Flumps to scoff on the way.' Lois loved Flumps. I was sure if I ate as many as she did, I'd look like an actual giant Flump, but she was all skinny-bummed and lanky.

'Aw, I really want to, but can't today, soz,' I said, stuffing my PE kit in my locker. 'I gotta meet my mum in town.' I didn't say anything about the doctor – I didn't really want to explain . . .

'Oh no, that's boring!' she groaned, sticking out her bottom lip, and making her eyes go all puppy-sad. She has these amazing eyes – huge and Smurf-blue. 'Can't you just tell your mum you've got something more important to do?' she teased.

'I wish! But maybe you can walk some of the way with me . . .' I began. I was thinking I could tell her about the magic as we went.

But right then her phone flashed silently in her hand.

'It's Bex,' she said, poking her screen. 'She wants to meet me . . . and, oh, here she comes now!'

Bex pushed through the double doors. She was only in Year Seven like us, but she was really tall, and had this layered, teenagery haircut and, when she could get away with it, loads of eyeliner – sometimes she looked like she was in about Year Nine. But she was *really* annoying – loud and showy-offy, and basically just trying to copy her big sister.

She wasn't friends with me at all, but she LOVED Lois. Their surnames started with the same letter, so they'd been sat next to each other in registration since the first day back in September.

But just in the last week or so, Bex had been hanging around Lois all the time. I was actually starting to worry that she was trying to take Lois away from me.

'Hey, Lo,' cried Bex, hugging her, and completely ignoring me. 'Wanna come over to mine now?'

'Um, OK,' said Lois. 'Yeah, yeah, cool.'

I looked at her, trying to work out if she meant it. Lois was always nice to *everyone*.

But she seemed to be smiling – like she really was pleased to go.

Ugh, well, I would *never* want to hang out with Bex . . . but maybe Lois actually liked her.

A little worry wriggled into my mind. Was Lois starting to get into more teenagery stuff like Bex these days, leaving me behind?

Lois was tugging her things out of her locker while Bex sat on the radiator, waiting, cracking gum and checking her face in a small mirror. She pulled out a pot of lipgloss from her pocket and smeared some on, and offered Lois the pot. Lois stuck her finger in and slicked some on her lips. It stank like cheap, party-bag sweets – proper sickly.

'Aw you're so pretty, babes,' cooed Bex. 'Hey, I know – why don't I give you a makeover at mine!'

Lois nodded. And smiled again – like she meant it.

I couldn't believe it. Lois had never bothered with make-up before. It wasn't her thing.

Or maybe it was now?

I realised I hadn't moved. I was just standing by my locker, shuffling about. I had to run now or Mum would be waiting.

I slammed my locker hard.

'Bye, Lois – I gotta rush,' I said, swinging my bag over my shoulder. I grinned at her, trying to be normal so she didn't see I was fed up. I didn't want her to think I was being silly or babyish.

'Oh, see you tomorrow, Courts,' she said, running to give me another hug.

I pushed through the doors and down the stairs, leaving Lois with Bex.

Grrrr . . . why didn't Bex just bog off?

I'd been just about to tell Lois all about the magic, but suddenly I wasn't sure if I wanted to any more. What if she thought it was kids' stuff, now she was trying to act all grown up like Bex?

I felt a lump in my throat coming. So as soon as I was outside the school gates, I started running. I ran as fast as I could all the way to the doctor's.

Chapter Eight

Mum was waiting outside for me. We rushed in the door just as the receptionist called my name.

It was the old-man doctor I didn't like very much – Dr Prop. He was a bit unfriendly and muttery, and used confusing, long words to tell you what was wrong with you. Me and Kyle had called him Dr Plop since we were little.

Mum did all the talking, but of course she missed out the most important bit – like, about the magic. Not that I wanted to tell the doctor anyway – obviously, no way. I could just tell that magic and Dr Plop didn't go together.

The doc let Mum finish, and then he scooted his wheely chair over to me. He listened to my heart with his doctor thingy and then he looked in my ears, down my throat and inside my eyes. Then he scooted his chair back to his desk really fast. I so wanted to have a go on that chair – it looked too fun.

Next he got me to lie down on his doctor bed, and he pressed my tummy about. All the time he was talking to Mum using his long, ploppy words. Then he looked at me.

'So can you tell me what happened just before you fainted, Courtney?' he said.

'I was feeling a bit funny, and my head was going round,' I said, shrugging. 'And then I just fell asleep . . . I mean, fainted.'

Mum took over. 'She's very stressed out at the moment, Doctor. Her grandmother's in hospital.' She lowered her voice. 'Quite bad . . .'

'So you were feeling anxious, Courtney?' the doctor asked.

I nodded. I thought about saying that it was also because Mum and Dad were yelling. But then I worried that he'd think they were rubbish parents or something and make me go and live in a children's home, so I didn't.

'Yes, about my gran,' I said firmly, not looking at Mum.

I got off the bed, and the doctor turned back to Mum again, and said loads of other stuff I didn't really get.

'. . . well, no signs of infections. We could take bloods for anaemia but there are no indications of that . . . blah, blah . . .'

Annie what?

'Really, these sound like classic panic attacks,' Dr Plop said, tapping his biro in his hand. 'So I think the best thing is to keep an eye on her for now. And try and keep her stress levels down.'

Panic attacks? Er, don't you mean amazing, fantabulous magic dreams, Dr Plop? Pah, he didn't know what he was talking about. And I actually reckoned my worry magic would be better than his clever-doctor medicines at curing people.

Like Gran . . .

I crossed all my fingers in my lap.

On Saturday . . .

We thanked the doc and left his room. As we went out the surgery doors, Mum put her arm around me.

'Well, there you go. Nothing too much wrong with you – we've just got to keep you calm,' she sighed. 'And we know what a worrywart you can be, so I really think . . .' She stopped –

'Oh hi, Ju!' she called out, waving at someone across the street. She stood on the kerb, mouthing stuff over the traffic and laughing. Mum always knew everyone in town.

Ugh, and there was that old *worrywart* thing again. People sometimes called me that, as if worrying was bad – like warts are bad. Well, I knew worrying did churn you up sometimes, but really it was dead useful – it helped you think of the bad stuff that might happen, so you were more *ready* . . .

Mum waved at her mate again and we walked on.

'So, where were we? Yes . . . er . . . but I hope you understand, darling, that this means you can't come and visit Gran,' Mum said, glancing down at me. 'It's bound to upset you too much seeing her so poorly.'

WHAAAAT?!!!!

'But, Mum, I have to!' I cried. She couldn't stop me seeing Gran . . . she couldn't do that!

Especially not now that I had my worry magic, which might actually help Gran get better.

'No, sorry, Courts – we have to be sensible. You heard what the doctor said.'

I started to moan, but as we turned a street corner, there was someone ELSE that Mum knew – Maddie, one of her friends from the sanctuary.

I groaned to myself.

'Oh hi, Donna,' said Maddie. 'Ah, this is lucky – I wanted to ask you about that new dog – you know, the lurcher . . .' They immediately started chatting on and on, so I was left just waiting again, with my hands in my pockets like a right twerp.

I scowled, and kicked an old squashed conker around on the leafy pavement.

How could Mum even *say* that I wasn't allowed to visit Gran?

The doc had gone and ruined everything, ploppy old him . . .

And I just hadn't seen this coming at all. I hadn't even worried about it.

I kicked the conker down a drain and it hit the water below. With a big plop.

Grrrr – it was all too *unfair*.

Chapter Nine

And even MORE annoying . . . when we got in, Dad *agreed* with Mum that I was banned from seeing Gran. It was just my luck . . . they never agreed on *anything* – but they were bezzie mates on this. *Doctor's orders*, they kept saying, *doctor's orders*.

Huh, well, *actually* the doctor's orders were to keep me calm. But they kept on shouting at each other and stressing me, didn't they – they forgot *that* part. They were only HALF listening to the doctor.

But there was no point in arguing. I could tell their minds were made up, so I didn't say anything. I just went to my room and cried.

After a bit, I wiped my face, sat up against my pillows and got out my felt tips, paper and my big horse book to lean on. I drew some angry, cartoony pictures of Mum and Dad, and then scribbled them out, before starting a letter to Gran. If I couldn't visit her, then I could at least write to her . . .

I did a border all round the edge of my paper and drew lots of Puddy cats, flowers and hearts. I wasn't much good at art so, to be honest, it was a bit rubbish and Year One-ish – and all the Puddys looked more like hippos than cats. But still, I knew Gran would like it.

Of course Puddy needed to sign it too. He was snoozing on my school uniform on my chair, so I crept over to him with my old blunt scissors and really carefully snipped a tiny bit of fur from his fluffy tummy. He rolled right over, stretching and purring. He didn't mind giving his fur to his granny-mum.

I Sellotaped the little wodge of fur onto the corner of Gran's letter, and labelled it 'Puddy-love'.

Then I wrote –

Dear Gran,

> *Mum and Dad say I can't visit you in case I get too upset, but I really want to . . . and it's not FAIR.*
> *So please get better and come home soon, Gran.*
> *I have so much to tell you.*
> *Me and Puddy miss you like mad, mad, MAD.*

Love from Courts xxxxxxxxxxx

A tear dripped off my nose and landed on the word 'SO'. I wiped it but the smudge made it look like the word was highlighted.

Well, it was true. I did have SO much to tell her . . .

I was definitely going to tell her about the magic. I had to tell someone, and I was sure that Gran would believe me, because she always GOT stuff.

Always.

Like, when other people said I was a worrywart, Gran never blamed me – she knew I couldn't help it. When I was at primary, she'd even invented this kind of game about worrying called 'Worry Wig'.

The whole thing started when I got this weird pyjama case from Auntie Jacq one Christmas. It was like a round, rainbow-striped cushion cover, made from extra-fluffy fun fur, and meant for keeping your night stuff in – but really, it was much better for wearing as a mad, dressing-up wig. For some reason, Gran began calling it the 'Worry Wig', and turned it into a game. Basically she said if I got worried about stuff, instead of fretting all day long, I had to zooooom my worries on pretend rockets all the way home, and into my Worry Wig on my bed for safekeeping.

Then in the evening I got a special Worry Wig Half-Hour when I could take my worries out, put on the wig if I wanted to, and worry as much as I liked – but only for those wiggy minutes.

Gran'd sit on my bed and say –

'Right, come on – give me them one by one.' So I'd tell her each worry, and she'd help me think of things I could do about it. Then after, she'd pretend to eat the worries all up: 'Yum, yum, that one was orange flavour. And another one? Oooh, chocolate mint. And that big one? Roast potato.' Often she'd make me laugh so much, I couldn't remember all the worries in the Wig.

I sighed.

But I hadn't played that since Gran had gone into hospital. I'd basically just worried 24/7 since then . . .

I kicked up my duvet and hooked my Worry Wig out from the bottom of my bed. It looked a bit tousled, like it was having a Bad Hair Day, so I shook it and smoothed out its fluff.

Anyway, maybe the Wig only worked on smaller stuff – like when I was worried about moving up into the junior playground or forgetting my Year Five play lines or something. But now I had BIG, fat worries – like Gran being ill and Mum and Dad splitting up . . .

I flopped back on my pillows. Puddy uncurled himself on the chair, arched his back, yawned, and came purring over to me, clawing my arms and nudging my hand, asking me to stroke him. I rolled over and snuffled him, and he flopped down on top of the Worry Wig.

I probably didn't even *need* a Worry Wig any more. Not now I had my stuuuuupendous Worry MAGIC.

Except I couldn't use it to help Gran if I was stupidly banned, could I?

Chapter Ten

I spent a while tidying my room – it always made me feel better doing that. I made a cosy nest on my bed out of my dressing gown for Puddy to sleep in, but he still liked the Worry Wig better.

Then I crept out to the loo. The house was silent. Which meant no one was fighting. Good . . .

But Kyle had made a huge mess in the bathroom when he'd had his bath after footie practice. All the towels were on the floor, and the tub was brown and gritty. Dad would blow his top if he saw the bathroom all mucky like that – Kyle was SO loser-ish.

Of course, there was no point in moaning at him – he wouldn't listen to me. So I just scrubbed the bath myself, and arranged the towels and shampoo how Dad liked them.

The airing cupboard door was half open, but when I pushed it, it wouldn't close. A massive bin liner had been stuffed onto the bottom shelf.

I unknotted it . . . it was bursting full of chewy dog toys – that squeezy, squeaking kind, and all shaped like roast chickens.

The bag had a handwritten price sticker on it – '£10 the lot'. Mum'd obviously bought them for the sanctuary from a charity shop or somewhere.

Argghhh. Ten quid was not much – but still enough to set Dad off like a firework. And what a dumb hiding place. He'd easily find them there.

I tugged at the bag and all the chickens squeaked inside as it came squashing out.

Where could I put them that Dad would NEVER look? My room was too small – no hiding places at all. And the garage was no good cos Dad was always fiddling about in there. Hmmm . . . Then I thought of the attic space in Mum and Dad's room. Dad probably never opened it – it was jam-packed with Mum's old jumbled-up stuff from years ago.

I sneaked out of the bathroom, holding the chicken bag behind my back.

I stopped for a second on the landing and listened. No one about . . .

But right then Kyle came stumbling out of his room.

'What's THAT?' he said, pointing. He still had mud on his face from footie practice even though he'd had a bath.

'Nothing,' I said. 'Just stupid stuff Mum's bought. I'm hiding it from Dad.'

He rolled his eyes. He was ALWAYS doing that these days. He couldn't look at me and keep his eyeballs still.

'You just don't learn, do you?' he hissed in a whisper. 'What's the point? They'll just argue about something else anyway. You seriously need to chill out . . .'

'Oh, shut up!' I snapped back. 'Just mind your own business!'

'Yeah, well, I'd say the same to you, Princess Perfect.'

I gave him an evil look, and barged past him into Mum and Dad's room. I tugged open the little door to the attic space, and stuffed in the squeaky bag. I could see why Mum hadn't hidden it in there – it was crammed full already. But I jammed the door shut with a chair, and hopped back out onto the landing. Big phew! Hopefully that had stopped THAT fight, at least. And this time without any worry magic!

Someone had put the telly on in the kitchen – probably Mum – and everything still seemed nice and calm. So I just whizzed back into my room and closed my door so Kyle couldn't come and get on my nerves again.

I got on with decorating Gran's envelope. I'd have to ask Dad to take it to her, I supposed.

But then there was a soft knock at the door, and Kyle stuck his head in.

'What?' I said, giving him a dirty look. 'Go away!'

'I can assure you that I don't want to talk to you either,' he said, pushing his glasses up his nose. 'But Mum said it's tea now.' He hesitated. 'And Dad's . . . er . . . gone out.'

My heart seemed to balloon in my chest. I caught my breath sharply and sat bolt upright. Dad never went out. Not unless there'd been trouble.

'Oh no . . . but when?'

'Don't get your knickers in a twist – he'll be back. I'm just warning you that he's not here for tea, that's all.'

'They had another fight, didn't they?' I said, pushing all my pens off my lap and scrambling up. 'What about?'

'I dunno, do I? I didn't even hear cos they were out in the garage. Probably just another pathetic shouting match about a pointless load of nothing.'

'Dad's probably just in his Shed,' I said, hoping.

'Nah, he flounced off, out the front . . .' Kyle curled his lip.

Ugh. Where had he *gone*?

My eyes started to prickle. And what was I doing, drawing in my room? I should've been downstairs ready to have a worry dream to make things better . . .

'Why didn't you come and TELL me they were fighting?' I said. 'I didn't even KNOW.'

Kyle gave me a scoffing look. 'Why would I do that? There's nothing YOU can do – duh!' And he just closed my door again.

Well, Kyle – yes, there is *actually*.

Chapter Eleven

I went down for tea.

Kyle was in the lounge, watching telly, and Mum was serving up. They both had grim faces, and no one mentioned Dad.

And even worse, tea was that old ham quiche from the day before. Yum.

While I waited, I nipped to the downstairs loo to see Henners. He lived in this huge, posh cage in there – Dad said it was 5-star deluxe.

I knelt down and fed him some raisins through the wire. He took them out of my fingers, and nibbled them with his whiskers twitching. Raisins were his complete favourite – they were like his sweeties – so I kept this secret store of them for him. Every time I had muesli for breakfast, I picked the raisins out and hid them behind a flowerpot in the kitchen. He never seemed to mind that they were a bit dusty.

'Courts!' Mum called. 'Tea's on the trays.' No one was in a chatty mood so we ate on our knees in front of the telly. We were halfway through when Dad clattered back through the front door.

I was on the chair nearest the lounge door, so I waved. He had a _misery_ face on, but he smiled hello to me as he took off his coat.

He slung it over the bottom of the banister, but as he did it, something fluttered out of his pocket onto the carpet. He didn't pick it up – he just stomped straight upstairs to his room.

I finished my tea quickly and told Mum I was going to bed to read. And on my way up, I stopped to pick up what Dad had dropped.

Oh, it was only a tissue . . .

But a pink flowery tissue . . . like, really, proper girlie. One of those posh ones out of a little packet that some ladies keep in their handbag. Mrs Eadie who played the piano for our primary school assemblies always had them.

Strange . . .

We didn't have any of that kind in our house. And Dad would never have bought tissues like that for himself. So where had he got it from?

My mind started speeding then.

I whipped up to my room and lay on my bed, chewing hard at my thumbnail.

Had Dad been to someone's *house*? But whose? Dad didn't have any friends nearby, and certainly not any ladies. Only Mum did.

My tummy flipped over suddenly.

Oh no – he didn't have a GIRLFRIEND, did he?

Maybe he'd found someone who didn't yell at him. Someone who looked like that weather girl on the telly he always whistled and giggled at.

Of course it took me ages to go to sleep with that thought in my head, and I was still worrying about it in the morning.

Chapter Twelve

The next day was Saturday. The day I was *supposed* to visit Gran. Before Dr Plop got me left out.

I knew Dad was going to the hospital later after he'd finished his garden work – or, huh, was he actually visiting his girlfriend?

I stomped downstairs, feeling really sulky. Dad had already gone and Mum was getting ready to go to her shift at the sanctuary. Well, at least I didn't have to worry about sorting out their silly fights for a few hours.

So I sat spooning in my cornflakes and texting Lois to check if she was still up for swimming. She sent me back a big YES and lots of smiley faces. Me and Lois were swimming-mad. We went together any time we could, but always every Saturday morning. We hardly ever missed it – it was like a regular thing, just us two.

The pool was only at the end of my road. Lois's house was in the wrong direction, but I usually went to call for her, otherwise I stood outside the pool waiting cos she was always late – she was so scatty.

It was cold, but there was a pretty, blue-and-white, stripy sky, and the sun was out. I was super-early so I took a long way round through the park and stopped for a quick swing, chucking my swimming bag down on the bench. Me and Lois had the same ones – bright yellow, thick plastic, see-through bags that looked like they were made out of lemon jelly. We loved them.

When I got to Lois's house, I knocked and her big brother Max flung open the door, wearing just jeans and holding a bowl of cereal. He cheesy-grinned at me under his floppy fringe.

'Aha, it's Naughty-Courty,' he said, through a mouthful.

'Hey, Max!' I stepped into the hall, giggling. Max was always a bit of a joker, and such a cool brother. Not like geeky Kyle, who was really quiet, and wore embarrassing, too-short joggers and computer-shop T-shirts.

Max turned and bellowed up the stairs –

'LO-O-O! Get down here.' He winked at me, and scuffed barefooted back into the kitchen.

Lois came hopping down, rubbing on some lip balm. I recognised that sickly, fruity smell straight away – she'd bought herself the same one as Bex! I felt myself tense up a bit, but Lois seemed so happy to see me, I managed not to frown.

She hooked her lemon-jelly bag off the hall pegs and we bowled out into the sunshine, and down the street, arm in arm, singing and larking about.

Oh, I loved Saturdays with Lois. Everything seemed easier when I was with her. I even forgot to worry . . .

But even as I thought that, my tummy tightened – oh dear, but maybe I *should* be worrying. It was weird – NOT worrying always worried me. In case things were going wrong without me realising . . .

I shook all that out of my mind. It was OK for a few hours. Mum and Dad weren't anywhere near each other. And Lois kept pushing me in puddles, so I had to think about THAT, or I was going to be soaking wet before we even got in the water.

It was quite busy at the pool, but we found a quieter corner, so we could play about. Swimming under each other's legs; throwing a coin for each other to collect from the bottom.

Then we played our favourite game – SHARKS! – which we'd invented that summer. The idea was to choose the most serious-looking swimmer and pretend they were a shark. It was always hilarious.

We picked this man with goggles and a funny moustache that made him look like he was doing that charity thing, Movember. He was swimming loads of lengths, and every time he came near us, we did these silent screams and swam away from him in a panic. Sometimes when we played it, people smiled. But this man just gave us the stink-eye, which made us laugh even more.

And all the time, I kept thinking how Lois seemed to have forgotten about being more grown up and boring like Bex. I was dead glad she wasn't . . . but I still wasn't ready to tell her about the magic. Not yet.

The sun started shining through the window, making bright patches on the water. So we floated on our backs in the sunshiney bits, watching the ripply reflection on the ceiling, and listening to the muffled noise of the pool. I always liked being in my own little world with my ears under the water. Everything felt softer and a long way away – sort of safe.

When we got cold, we climbed out and had our usual long, hot showers, using loads of Lois's strawberry shampoo. Then we blasted our heads under the big driers and plaited each other's hair. It was our routine and it always felt kind of comforting. And because we both had long, brown hair, people sometimes thought we were twins – even though we looked nothing alike – which always made us giggle.

'I'm *starving*,' said Lois, after. She said that every week.

So we queued up at the machine to get some crisps. Only salt and vinegar would do after swimming.

In the queue me and Lois messed around, doing our Dementor faces, practising for Halloween.

'Mwahahahaha!' Lois pulled down her bottom eyelids, screwed up her face and leered at me.

She was really pretty, but she could pull the *worst* mean faces.

'Argh, you actually look like Voldemort,' I squealed. 'Look – you're even scaring the children!'

A toddler with chocolate around his face was peeping up at her from behind his mum's legs while his mum nattered to her friend. His lip was wobbling and he looked proper terrified.

'Oh no!' said Lois. She couldn't bear upsetting anyone. She bent down and flashed the boy her biggest, friendliest smile. 'It's OK – it was only a game,' she said gently. He grinned back at her then, all chocolatey teeth.

'Come on, get your ugly mug out of here before you make anyone else cry,' I said, pushing her towards the doors and out into the cold. We were still laughing, stuffing down our crisps, and dawdling along the road when –

'LOISSSSSS!' cried a voice from behind us. 'I'm, like, soooooo made up to see you.'

We turned and it was Bex.

I sighed quietly to myself.

Oh, not YOU . . .

She was wearing skinny jeans and a teenagery top that showed her tummy, and was carrying two huge bags of shopping.

'My mum *made* me go to the shop for her, but I'm so staying out with you now,' she said, dropping the bags so they crashed onto the pavement and bouncing up to Lois.

Oh right . . . invite yourself along then.

And she still hadn't even looked at me.

'You been swimming? You shoulda told me cos I got this new bikini!' She did this model pose with her hand behind her head. 'I'll come with you next time.'

WHAT?!! Swimming was mine and Lois's special thing we did, just us. No way did I want *her* coming.

But Lois smiled and nodded.

'Yeah . . . um . . . OK,' she said.

I widened my eyes at Lois – like, *Uh?* – and gave a tiny shake of my head. But she sort of made an awkward face and shrugged.

She literally couldn't say no to anyone – even if she wanted to.

Unless she really DID want Bex to come – secretly.

My worries started worming back.

Maybe Lois was getting bored of Saturdays with just me. Tired of our old kiddy games . . .

I chewed my lip and followed behind them.

And then Bex managed to say something which got on my wick EVEN more.

'Oh, and I love your yellow bag, Lois – it's lush! Where'd you get it? I want one too!'

OMG.

Why didn't she just GO AWAY!

Chapter Thirteen

But of course Bex *didn't* go away.

She stuck to us like bubblegum, all along the street towards my house.

I'd wanted to ask Lois round for lunch, seeing as Mum and Dad were out for a bit. But Bex wasn't coming to mine – that was for sure.

How was I going to get rid of her?

But when we passed the park gate Bex started up –

'Oh, come in the park with me, Lo,' she begged. 'I'm bored out of my mind at home. I'll text my mum and say I'll bring the shopping laters. Yeah?'

'Er . . . OK,' said Lois, looking at me like she wanted me to come too. 'But I gotta go in a while cos my mum's making me go to my little cousin's birthday party.'

I wasn't letting Bex push me out, so I had to go with them.

The sun had brought tonnes of people to the park. Toddlers and prams. People sat outside the cafe. Some older boys were playing football using jumpers as goals, and a group of Year Ten girls I recognised were sitting on a bench, shouting stuff to the football boys. It felt almost like summer, not October.

We lazed about on the swings for a while, swinging as high as we could and hanging upside down so our hair swept the floor. Bex kept standing on her swing to peep over the wall into a garden, because apparently some boy called Dominic Butler she liked in Year Eight lived there.

One time she thought she saw him come into his garden. She screamed, ducked down and pretend-fell off her swing.

Lois laughed, but I didn't actually think it was that funny at all.

After that, we flopped about on the bench, sort of sunbathing, and wolfing down a pot of Flumps Lois had in her bag.

Bex had managed to squeeze her bum in between me and Lois, and just chattered on non-stop, showing off about how she was going to get a nose piercing, and maybe even a tattoo. Obviously it was all rubbish – she SO wasn't allowed.

I tried to catch Lois's eye, but she always seemed to be looking at Bex.

Why?

'Hey, Lo,' said Bex, 'so when d'you want to come to mine again and watch more *Vampire WAGS?*'

I felt my eyebrows fly up. They'd watched that without me . . . and Lois hadn't said.

'Yeah, we got through nearly the whole first series yesterday,' said Bex, actually speaking to me for once, and looking well pleased with herself. 'It was amazies, wasn't it, Lo?'

'Um, yes . . .' began Lois, glancing at me

quickly. 'But, Courts – of course, we missed you . . . Remember you had to go and meet your mum, so you couldn't stay out?'

I gave her a tiny smile, digging my heels into the dirt. 'Yeah, yeah – it's fine,' I muttered.

But the whole thing was totally bugging me. Lois must have spent nearly ALL evening with Bex, then. So maybe I'd been right to worry – perhaps Lois really *was* starting to like Bex more than me . . .

I felt tears begin to pool in my eyes, and I quickly blinked them away.

Then suddenly Bex threw her arms up, proper drama-queen style.

'Hey, HEY, guys!' she said, cracking her gum. 'I just had this mega idea. Let's play Truth or Dare!'

'Um . . . OK!' said Lois, grinning.

But I shook my head hard.

'Oh, why not, Courtney?' said Bex, tutting. 'Me and Lois both want to . . . it'll be super LOLZ.'

I shook my head harder. I just knew playing a game like that with Bex would be horrible.

'Looks like it's me and you playing, then, Lo,' said Bex. She turned her back so she was blocking me out.

She was so trying to get rid of me. Well, it wasn't going to work . . .

'OK, I'll play,' I sighed.

'I'm FIRST!' cried Bex. Obviously . . .

'Truth or Dare?' said Lois, clapping her hands.

'Truth!' said Bex. 'And my truth is . . . I think Dominic Butler is lush!'

Lois giggled. 'Well, we kinda knew that already . . .'

'No, but Dom is my one true *love*,' she said, clutching her heart. 'Bex Butler . . . does it sound nice?'

Lois laughed again, but I didn't.

Since when was Lois interested in talking about *boys*? She was just copying Bex.

Huh, next time I hoped Bex would choose dare. Then I'd dare her to stick her head down a toilet and leave it there for a week.

'My turn!' said Lois, bouncing on her bum. 'Give me a dare!'

'Oh yeah, Lo-Lo!' said Bex. 'OK, hang on . . .' She sat thinking.

'I've got one!' I said. 'Lois – I dare you to walk right into the middle of those boys playing footie, and do the splits!'

Lois roared with laughter. 'Oh please, no!'

'Or you have to put your shoes on the wrong feet, and ask one of them for a Gangnam Style dance-off,' I said, giggling too.

Lois roared again. 'I'm not doing that either . . . but you're so funny, Courts!'

Bex curled her top lip. She didn't like Lois thinking I was funny. Not one little bit.

'No, I've got a *better* idea,' Bex said. 'I double-dare you to pretend to be sick. Make a sicking-up noise and pour water out of your bottle from behind your head. Then everyone will think it's true!'

'No way, gross!' shrieked Lois. 'Do I have to?'

'YES! said Bex. And of course, Lois did what Her Majesty Bex said.

She stood up, bent over, and held her water bottle behind her face. She made a small, gagging noise and poured a tiny splash of water onto the grass. But then she just started laughing, and fell back down next to us.

'How *embarrassing*,' she squealed, her face bright red. 'Was everyone staring at me?'

'No, you're all right – no one even saw,' I said.

'Phewee!' she said.

I smiled at her. But to be honest, she hadn't done her dare properly at all.

'Right,' said Bex, turning to me. 'We've both done ours. Now YOU!' I didn't like the way she said 'YOU'. 'Truth or dare, *Courtney*?'

'Nothing or nothing,' I said, swivelling away.

'You have to choose – it's the game,' Bex said.

'Oh, go on, Courts,' said Lois. 'Choose dare – it's wicked. And I'll think of a fun one for you.'

'OK,' I sighed. 'Dare.'

Bex looked at me and sucked in her cheeks. I knew she was thinking up some mean things. I turned to Lois for her dare, but she hadn't thought of one yet.

Then Bex grinned. 'Got it!'

She dug into her shopping bags, and pulled out a box of Frubes – those yoghurt-in-a-tube things.

'These are for my little brother, but he won't miss one. So . . .' She looked at me and sniggered. 'I dare you to go over to those girls at the bench, drop this and jump on it hard . . . so it squirts out all over them!'

WHAT? Frube some Year Ten girls? That'd be like shaking a killer-wasps' nest, and Bex knew it.

Lois smiled nervously, and made an uh-oh face at me.

'I'm not doing it!' I said.

But Lois didn't say anything. Why wasn't she sticking up for me?

'You have to,' said Bex. 'We did our dares.' Then she did another over-the-top sigh, and just threw the Frube back into her bag. 'Oh, whatever – you're just SO *boring*, Courtney.'

That was it.

I'd had enough of Bossy Bex.

'All right,' I said. I took the Frube back out of the bag and stood up. I made out like I was walking off towards the group of girls. Then I stopped, threw the Frube down next to Bex, and stamped on it. Whoa, so much yoghurt in one wincy tube!

But instead of Frubing Bex's annoying, cowbag face, it squirted the wrong way.

Completely the wrong way . . .

All over Lois . . . her top, her jeans and her long plait. She was covered.

'What d'you do THAT for, you idiot?' squawked Bex.

Lois just stared down at herself in horror, before turning and gawping up at me.

'Oh, sorry, Lo! I didn't mean to . . .' I cried.

'But why did you . . . ?' squeaked Lois. She tried to wipe her jeans with her hand, but the yoghurt was so thick and slimy, she just smeared it and made it worse. 'Oh no, I'm going to stink!'

'Yuck – and that looks *bad*. You look like you actually did vom over yourself!' said Bex. 'And you gotta walk home past all those boys like that.'

'Yes . . . oh NO, I look SO disgusting, don't I?' said Lois, getting teary. She got really embarrassed about stuff like that.

Bex put her arm round Lois, and gave me a smug look. 'I can't believe you, Courtney – that was harsh!'

'I'm sorry! Soooo sorry,' I stammered, trying to get Lois to look at me. But she was too busy scraping her top with some grass.

She was SO peed off with me.

'Come on, Lois – let's go to the loo and TRY and clean it off,' said Bex, shooting me a you-loser look. 'But I don't think it's going to come off easily.'

Huh, she was loving this. LOVING it . . .

Lois nodded and got up.

I stayed where I was. Lois didn't seem bothered whether I came or not.

'Sorry again,' I muttered, miserably. I felt a big lump rise in my throat.

Lois smiled weakly and half waved, but Bex whispered to her and pulled her away by her arm.

I sat back down on the bench by myself, and watched them go into the loo block.

Oh no, oh no. My heart was thumping really fast and my tears came properly then.

I pulled my hood up and bent over, so no one could see my face. But my teardrops were making dark marks on my jeans.

How stupid could I be . . .

I'd just Frubed my best friend. And now she probably hated me . . . and would go off with Bex.

And right then that funny feeling started creeping through me.

The feeling I was starting to know well.

Spinny.

Floppy.

Heavy . . .

Oh, the worry magic!

My face lolled forward on my chest . . .

Asleep again.

Chapter Fourteen

The dream was a wild tumble.

Flashes of faces. Lois smiling at me, holding my hand. A Slush Puppie. Bex pouting with bright blue lips. And then the lovely calmness as the dream faded away.

'Courts?' Lois was suddenly back, bending over me, panting from running.

My eyes popped open.

Er . . . what was going on? I shook myself . . .

Then I remembered.

Oh no, the Frube . . . !

I eyed Lois up and down. She still looked pretty smeary.

'Er . . . so sorry again about . . . you know,' I muttered, rubbing my eyes.

'Oh . . . never mind,' said Lois, sitting down next to me on the bench, taking my hand and smiling a big smile. 'Don't worry. I don't really care – let's forget it.'

And right then my dream whooshed back to me. Oh wow – the magic had worked on Lois too?

'Where's Bex?' I said, looking all around.

'Oh, she's just getting a Slush Puppie from the cafe.'

I nodded.

Of course.

And I knew what colour it would be . . .

I turned and watched Bex jogging over to us, holding a cup of blue slushy ice with a straw in.

'I'd better keep this away from you, Courtney, in case you, like, THROW it at someone,' she sneered, sitting down again. She wasn't pretending to be even a little bit nice to me any more.

But Lois nudged her. 'Let's leave it now, eh,'

Lois muttered, blushing.

Bex's mouth dropped open in surprise around her straw. Her lips and tongue had gone blue like a sea monster's.

I knew it wasn't easy for Lois to stand up to Bex, but the magic was making her do it.

'Yeah, well . . .' began Bex, pouting all blue.

Lois shook her head at her.

'No, really, can we just drop it?' she said, her face nearly the colour of her red hoodie.

Wow. Lois hated arguments, but she was really sticking up for me!

Bex looked gobsmacked.

'Whatevs,' she said, flicking her hair and glaring at the floor. 'I'm off now anyhow. Gotta take the shopping back to my mum.'

She got up and grabbed the shopping bags, tossing her head and acting up all hurt.

'I'll text you later, Bex,' called Lois.

But Bex didn't reply. She kicked the gate open with her foot and never looked back.

'Uh-oh, whoops!' winced Lois. 'I expect she'll come round.'

I wanted to say that I really hoped NOT. But I just nodded.

Bad luck, Bex. Three really is a crowd. And I've got lovely, *lovely* worry magic on my side.

And the best thing was that the magic seemed to work on *everybody*, not just Mum and Dad!

Which meant it would definitely work on Gran, wouldn't it . . .

I was sure now.

Chapter Fifteen

Lois had to rush off to her cousin's party, so I went home.

Mum and Dad weren't there when I got in.

I was just taking off my shoes when . . .

Ting-a-ling-a-ling . . . Ting-a-ling-a-ling . . .

Uh? An ice-cream van in our street? Oh wow, we NEVER got them down our way normally! Especially not this time of year.

Kyle swung down the banister like a chimp. He was still wearing his sweaty sports clothes from his morning run. Yuck.

'Double choc Magnum, you're mine!' he said, as he raced past me and flew out of the door.

'Quick, stop it!' I shouted, scooting down the path after him. 'Don't let it go by.'

Ting-a-ling-a-ling-a-ling!

The ice-cream van pulled up right outside our house, blocking the whole road. It coughed out some black smoke, and then the engine conked out. But the ice-cream music just kept on *ting-a-ling*ing at top volume.

The van was the small, old-fashioned kind. Seriously old. Like its windows could fall out any minute and squash you. Or its ice creams would make you die of mould.

'Ewww!' I said.

'Mum!' gasped Kyle, pointing.

'Mum?' And then I saw what he meant. Mum was driving the van.

Mum was an ice-cream lady? But since when?

She got out, beaming at us.

'Do you like it, then?' She had to shout over the ice-cream music.

'What d'you mean?' I yelled back.

'It's ours!' cried Mum. 'Our own ice-cream van!'

Me and Kyle looked at each other. Kyle shook his head, walked over, opened the driver's door and got in. There was a loud whacking noise and the *ting-a-ling*ing stopped.

A lady and her toddler had come down the street to buy an ice cream. But she took one look at the grimy old van, and hurried away again while her kid screamed in her arms.

Kyle came back over to us, his face all straight and hard. I knew my face looked like that too.

'The exhaust's definitely gone. And the piston rings too, by the look of all that smoke,' he said in his flat, fact-man voice. As usual, I didn't know how he knew about stuff like that, but I totally believed him.

It was like Mum hadn't even heard him.

'Isn't it retro and FAB?' she gabbled. 'You just have to use your imagination! It's going to be my mobile dog-wash, see. A poodle parlour on wheels, so I can take my salon to my clients' doors! I really don't know why I haven't thought of this as a career before. I mean, I'm good with animals AND I'm a hairdresser, so it'll be dead easy.'

Me and Kyle gave each other a tired look.

OMG, Mum was SO NOT a hairdresser. She'd started a course years ago when she was seventeen, but somehow she never remembered that she'd dropped out after one term because she was RUBBISH. She'd always cut our hair when we were little – me and Kyle kept the photos hidden at the back of the cupboard.

It was so silly that I half wanted to laugh. Except I knew Dad would NOT see the funny side. And he hated any dogs coming to the house cos they always sniffed Henners' cage and scared him.

'But, Mum! Dad won't like dogs coming round . . .'

'But that's the whole point!' Mum cried. 'They WON'T come to the house once the van is done up and ready – they'll be in there! And I think I could make some serious cash – I've already got three customers lined up. Janet Carter wants me to do her new rescue dog, Derek, ASAP.'

'But . . . but . . . what about the money to buy this?' I stammered. My head was full of too many things to worry about all at once. 'Dad said . . .'

'A hundred and fifty quid – that's all,' said Mum. 'A total bargain, I reckon. And I haven't even paid up front. I gave the car-mender man £50 – and he said I can pay him the rest when I can.'

'Yeah, well, he saw you coming. I wouldn't pay fifteen pence for THAT rust bucket,' muttered Kyle.

Mum ignored him again.

'Just come in and look!' she said, practically skipping to the van's back door.

We followed her. The back door was so rusted up we had to wrench it open. Inside it was still kitted out like a proper ice-cream van, with a freezer and a Mr Whippy machine and stuff.

Mum waved us up the steps, and we all three squeezed inside.

It stank like old cheese and sick.

Kyle opened the freezer and we peered in. At the bottom were some defrosted ice poles, lying curled up in a pool of water. They looked like strange, colourful, dinosaur worms.

'No one's even cleaned it out!' I said, holding my nose.

'Nothing a bit of scrubbing won't sort,' said Mum. 'I imagine a dog-clipping table here.' She waved her arms about, pointing. 'A dog bath there . . . and maybe it could even double up as a weekend camper van. Dad could build pull-down bunk-beds here . . .'

'And full-sized swimming pool over here?' I said, pointing to the tiny sink.

'Mum – there's not room for even one bed,' said Kyle, flatly. 'It's stupid.'

'Beds for elves perhaps,' I said, and Kyle sniggered.

I don't know why I was joking. It wasn't funny.

'No, there'll be lots of space with the freezer gone,' insisted Mum, looking hurt.

I just wanted to shout at her, but I knew it was pointless. Instead I just chewed my cuff and worried. This was bad. This was VERY bad. Almost as bad as the pig.

'Oh, get over the long faces – this is a cool plan!!' said Mum. 'And I don't have to tell Dad about it straight away. I can wait until until I've done a few practice dogs. Then I'll wave some money under his nose, and he'll be happy too!'

'Yeah, like he won't notice a ginormous ice-cream van parked out the front,' said Kyle, shoving his hands into his pockets.

But Mum's face was set firm. I knew she wasn't going to be talked out of this.

I sighed. 'Maybe you can hide it, Mum? Like, in the sanctuary car park?' I knew that was probably just storing up trouble for later, but it was all I could think of.

Mum nodded, beaming at me and still yacking on, as we hopped out of the smelly van.

'I can't wait to get started, actually. In fact I'll ring Janet and get her new dog booked in right away. He can be my trial run! My guinea pig-dog!'

'What – today?' I said. 'Here?

'Don't look so worried, Courts. I'll do it on the garden table. And . . .' Mum nudged me. 'I'll wait till tomorrow morning when Dad's out doing his old lady's garden. He'll never even know.'

We all stood looking at the van. The horrid thing had *Mr Whippy* painted across the side, except the *W* had rubbed off, so it just said *Mr hippy*. Dad was going to love that too.

Dad the Hippy. Not.

All I could think of was Dad's face when he saw it. And then his face going even darker as Mum explained how he would be building beds for elves inside.

Then I wanted to cry.

Cars were tooting in the road. The van was blocking both ways.

Mum ran and jumped into the van. It puffed out loads of fumes, and sounded like it was in terrible pain, but it just about started up. The music started too, but instead of going *ting-a-ling*, it got stuck on one high, sharp *tiiiiiiiiiiiiiiiiiiiiiiiiiiiing*.

I could see Mum hitting the dashboard, and finally the noise stopped. Then she pulled into the neighbour's driveway, and the cars all drove past in an angry, fast way.

'I'll take it straight to the sanctuary car park now,' she called to us over the engine. She tapped her finger on the side of her nose, like it was all a fun secret, and drove off in a cloud of choking black smoke.

Chapter Sixteen

The evening went off OK – everyone seemed too tired even to pick a fight for once.

And Dad got Henners out for a play, which always put him in a better mood.

Once the pretty weather girl came on the telly, and I watched Dad hard from behind my hair. But he didn't even look at her that time – he only had eyes for Henners.

Well, if I'd worried right and Dad really did have a girlfriend, she'd never beat Henners . . . so bad luck to horrid her.

Next morning Dad went off to do his Sunday garden job.

I knew Mum had arranged for Derek to come straight round. So maybe – just maybe – Derek would be all poodled and gone by the time Dad got back.

I stayed in my room, worrying and plaiting and re-plaiting my hair until the doorbell went. I heard voices and when the front door closed, I ran down, catching Mum up in the kitchen on her way towards the garden. She had a small, white, fluffy dog on a lead.

'Oh this is Derek, Courts, isn't he a cutie?' said Mum.

Derek took one look at me, and started snarling so much that Mum had to use all her weedy muscles to drag him off me.

Yeah, what a cutie. Apart from his face full of gnashing teeth. And his bad-lad attitude.

My heart sank. I didn't think Derek was going to be easy to poodle.

I followed them out. It was cold and misty. Hardly dog-bubble-bath weather.

'Yeah, so Derek is Janet's new rescue dog – our first customer,' said Mum brightly over the racket, still pretending he was a normal dog. 'I'm sure he'll settle down in a mo – and then we can start on his fur cut and bath.' She nodded her head towards an old plastic baby bath filled with water in the middle of the lawn.

What?! Did Mum seriously reckon she was going to bath him in that? Without losing some fingers or maybe her entire life? And I didn't like that 'we' . . .

Mum was just cooing down at Derek about how he was going to look gorgeous, when he suddenly flew into the air, barking like crazy at a pigeon. He yanked so hard on his lead that it pulled completely out of Mum's hand and he legged it off across the lawn.

'Oh, the little tyke!' cried Mum.

He circled the garden, his lead trailing behind him, and came pelting towards us, growling and slobbering.

'Here, Derek! Good boy,' sang Mum. She bent down and tried to grab him. But he snapped at her, swerved and scarpered, using the bathtub as a sort of mini roundabout.

'Derek! SIT! HEEL!' Mum ordered.

But Derek just did another *ha-ha-can't-catch-me!* lap of the garden, ran onto Dad's veg plot and started doing loads of speedy little wees on everything. It was like he was trying to cock his leg on every *single* vegetable. How did his tummy have room for so much wee?

Then he finished off with a great big poo right on top of a cabbage.

Ewww! Thank goodness Dad wasn't here to see THAT . . .

I stood chewing my nails and watched Mum chase Derek off the veg. She pulled a bag out of her pocket, and put the whole cabbage and poo in it, wrinkling up her nose.

The she got back to trying to rugby-tackle Derek. He was SO winning. It was like watching one of those falling-over-a-banana-skin, pie-in-your-face comedy shows on telly. But I couldn't laugh cos my eyes kept darting up at the dark clouds.

I'd forgotten to worry about RAIN. Dad *should* be at work all morning but if it looked like it was going to tip down, he might just knock off early. Oh pleeeease don't come back yet, Dad. It looked like Derek was going to be a *very* long job.

'Blimey, he's fast,' sighed Mum, stopping to catch her breath, holding her knees. 'Can you just give us a hand, Courts?' she puffed, as Derek blasted past again, growling doggy swear words. 'And when we've got him, could you help me dunk him in the bath . . . and then hold him on the garden table while I give him a quick trim? That be OK?'

I just looked at her, speechless. Was she mad? Did she want her only daughter to become an actual dog's dinner?'

'I know it's tricky, but we've got to try,' she breathed. 'I promised Janet I'd give him a jolly good wash at the very least . . . because honestly, he really, *really* smells.'

Smells. Bites. Poos . . . Yay for Derek. Double yay that Derek was at our house. Good one, Mum.

And then the rain started.

I pulled my coat round me, and watched Derek cock his leg and wee into his own bath, and then do some proud backwards kicks.

The rain was getting heavier.

Mum was still warbling on – 'You just have to try and understand him. Poor Derek's had such a bad time. So many owners have brought him back to the sanctuary.' She shook her head like it was hard to believe. 'Janet kindly offered to give him a fresh start, but she'll be so worried if she finds out he's been naughty for me too.'

NAUGHTY?! Derek was a gremlin in a cute dog costume.

'Oh no – look what's he doing *now!*' I cried, pointing. 'Derek – NO!'

He was digging a hole under the fence, sending a huge spray of dirt over all Dad's kalc. I ran and dived at him, but he scrambled away from me. He sort of bounced off the fence, and belted off like a snooker ball in a straight line towards . . .

OH NO . . .

I suddenly realised what he was aiming for.

Dad's precious Shed!

With its comfy chair, radio, neat boxes of seeds and tools.

The door was wide open . . .

I flew into a sprint, the rain pelting in my face.

Why had Mum even gone in there? No one was supposed to.

Maybe she'd borrowed Dad's scissors? But why hadn't she shut the stupid door?!

My shoes kept skidding on the damp grass, but me and Derek were neck and neck. He was eyeballing me and slavering at the mouth as he raced me.

He beat me by a nose, and screeched to a stop, his leg already cocked.

I grabbed hold of him by the scruff, but wee just spouted out of him . . . onto Dad's tool bag . . . chair cushion . . . open packet of flapjacks . . .

UGH!

Derek was all foam and teeth. I dropped him and pushed him out of the shed with a broom, and he hurtled away.

I turned round. And my heart grew in my chest and then pinged back to its normal size.

Dad.

Standing by the gate.

And I could tell from his face that he'd seen the whole Weeing-in-the-Shed show, every lovely moment of it.

Suddenly the energy ran out of me and my legs felt weird and jellyish. I caught hold of the shed door as I wobbled on my feet.

Dad was stalking across the lawn to Mum, pointing at his shed.

'DONNA!' he barked. 'How COULD you . . . ?'

Mum gabbled some words about dog-clipping and money. But Dad was gripping his bald head so hard he was making white marks.

'No, no, NO! That dog just PEED in my shed! On my flapjacks.' Dad's voice was squeaking with not-believing-it. 'Why was the door even open?!'

My heart was doing back flips.

Dad would just storm off again now!

And stay out. *Somewhere* . . .

And he didn't even KNOW about the junk ice-cream van yet.

My head spun and my eyes went shadowy.

I tipped forward on my feet, nearly stumbling over. So I crouched down, panting.

Ooh, giddy . . .

I toppled and sank down . . . down . . . down onto the damp leaves.

Musty, soggy . . . wet soaking into my jeans . . . rain drumming on my back.

I thumped flat down on the ground. Out cold.

Chapter Seventeen

The worry dream was a whizzy one. It charged through my head, but I still caught some pictures . . . Mrs Carter at our door, collecting a yapping Derek. Mum holding a yellow spray bottle. And Dad cooking his famous yummy pancakes.

I woke up, shivering, and sat up. Some leaves had stuck to my cheek so I plucked them off, my ears ringing with Derek still barking, barking, barking his bonce off.

Dad pulled me to my feet.

'There you go now, Courts,' Dad said. 'You're all right now.'

I could see Mum hauling Derek by his lead over to the garage. She shoved him in and tugged the door closed quickly behind him. Then she literally ran over to us, peering at me, all white again.

'Oh, Courts, are you OK?' she said, brushing more leaves out of my hair. 'Oh dear, oh no – it happened again!'

'Back to the doctor, I think, if this panic thing goes on much longer,' said Dad. And Mum nodded.

'Oh no!' I said. 'I'm really fine . . .'

But they weren't listening. They were too busy whisking me indoors, holding me up either side as if I might just slip through a crack in the ground.

They fussed me onto the sofa. Then I just lay back and watched my worry dream come true before my eyes again. It was the best thing ever, as usual – like being at the cinema. All I needed was some popcorn.

First, Mum rang Mrs Carter, and before long, she turned up at our door. Mum got Derek from the garage, and Mrs Carter led him away, still dirty and fluffy and still doing his nut barking.

Hooray! Magic – 1; Derek – nil.

Then Mum came over to me, tucked me under her blanket, and said she was just nipping out to the Shed to clean it. I nodded because of course, I knew this was going to happen already. And I knew which cleaning spray she would use too – the yellow one under the sink, just like in my dream.

Next Dad popped his head round the lounge door.

'Hungry, Courts? Because guess what I'm making for a special treat?!' He waggled his eyebrows at me.

'Pancakes!' I said.

He pulled a surprised face. 'Hey, I'm impressed! How'd you guess?'

'Oh, I dunno – I must have dreamt it!' I said. Ha, Dad would think I was joking, but 'course I wasn't. Not one bit.

He winked at me and went off to the kitchen.

I grinned to myself. 'Yummy – thanks, Dad,' I called after him.

Ahh, magic – you did it again! You fixed *everything, a*nd you got me pancakes – my favouritest things ever.

The only bad thing was Dad talking about the doctor again. There was nothing wrong with me! In fact, there was a whole LOT *right* with me. My worry magic was the coolest – I didn't want to be cured, no way. Not that Dr Plop would have any get-rid-of-magic pills, but I still didn't want to deal with any more of his meddling.

I pulled a blanket over myself, scowling about Dr Plop, when suddenly something zipped into my head . . . The next day was Lois's birthday! I needed to sort out her pressie! But with all this stuff going on, I'd nearly forgotten. How *could* I?

I went up to my room and pulled some wrapping paper out of my drawer.

I'd got Lois a giant pack of gummy bears. They were her favourite sweets after Flumps, and I'd always got her a bag since Infants.

But now, when I looked down at the packet, I wasn't so sure any more. Maybe it was way too primary-school-ish as a present. I wasn't twelve until May, so Lois was older than me by quite a few months. Maybe she'd prefer something a bit older . . .

I made a face at the gummy bears, but they'd have to do – I didn't have anything else.

I wrapped the bears up, and put them in my school bag.

Chapter Eighteen

Everyone was crowding around Lois before first lesson the next day.

I wriggled in close to her and handed her my present.

'Happy birthday! I hope it's not too babyish now you're twelve!' I whispered.

She hugged me, feeling the parcel and giggling. 'No way – gummy bears forever and ever!'

But then Bex arrived – and made this big entrance, of course.

'BIRTHDAY GIRL!' she shrieked. She barged

her way through to Lois, so I got pushed out to the outside of the group. Then she pulled a present out from behind her back – like, *ta-daaah!*

It was wrapped up all glam, with a big purple bow.

'Oh wow – thanks!' said Lois, looking a bit stunned.

Inside was this bracelet in its own velvet box. Proper posh. And not at all babyish.

'That's SO gorgy!' said Martha B.

And Lois was all wow-thanks, wow-thanks over and over again.

It was SO annoying.

'Yeah, it's designer,' said Bex. Pah, she reckoned!

I was glad when Lois finally put the dumb bracelet away and showed us the wicked new phone she'd got for her birthday. She played us different ringtones, keeping an eye out for Miss Cave. All the teachers were really bossy about phones in our school – but Miss Cave was our tutor as well as our English teacher, and was extra strict with us about EVERYTHING. And quite scary. Which is why everyone called her Cave

Woman, even though she was old and small, and often wore pink.

'Hey, listen to my text alert – it's my big bro thinking he's funny!' Lois held the phone up, and we could hear Max *quack-quack-quack*ing.

We all sniggered. Funny old Max.

'Can I have a look?' I asked, and Lois handed me her phone. It was posh – nicer than mine by miles.

'Hey, birthday piccie of us two,' I said. Lois put her head next to mine and we grinned. But when we looked at the picture, only Lois laughed. Because there just above us was Bex's stupid face, sticking out her tongue . . . she'd totally photobombed us! I couldn't even be in a photo by myself with Lois without Bex muscling in!

'Oh, let me take one of *me* and the birthday girl now,' said Bex, reaching to snatch the phone.

'I haven't finished looking yet,' I said, turning away from her.

Bex gave me a sharp look – we'd both totally given up pretending to be even a bit friends.

'Quiet please, Year Seven. Line up by the door.' Cave Woman had arrived.

I stuffed Lois's phone into her bag, and we all scuffled in.

Cave Woman had one of those pointless boy-girl seating plans. Lois was down the front next to pain-in-the-butt Kai Brown. I was at the back next to Toby G, who ground his teeth and sniffed all lesson. And – worse luck – Bex was right in front of me next to sweaty Aaron. English was such fun . . .

But we were doing creative writing – my favourite. And we were supposed to be working quietly by ourselves. But Bex kept whispering to Aaron, and she was getting away with it too, because Cave Woman was actually quite deaf. Her cave-woman ears were probably too full of fur.

Bex was showing off to Aaron. Her top hobby.

'I'm probs going to see a 15 film later,' she said. 'You know, that new one with Rupert Grint in it.'

Her whisper was so loud I could hear every word, but Aaron wasn't even listening – I could see his pen going across his page.

'I always get into 15s, easy . . . I just tell them my sister's birthday and they believe me . . .'

Fair play to her – she had a talent for ridiculous boasting.

She twirled her hair round her pen. 'Yeah, maybe I'll ask Lois to come with me after school . . .'

WHAT?!

I wanted to see Lois after school! We always did something together on our birthdays. Bex could get lost! She was bang out of order . . . as usual.

I shot a glance at Cave Woman. She was typing on her laptop, not looking my way.

I sneaked my phone out of my bag.

I would never do something like this usually – I was always too worried about getting in trouble. But this was an emergency!

I held my phone under the table and wrote a speedy text to Lois, peeping up at Cave Woman at every other word. If she saw me, my life would be over. She would feed me to her pet tyrannosaurus.

SEE YOU STR8 AFTER SCH, LO-LO? JUST U AND ME 4 B'DAY STUFF? OR A SWIM?xx

I looked over at Lois before I sent it. She was head-down, working away, but I hoped she'd sneak a peek at her new phone before the end of the lesson.

I hit SEND . . .

Ha, good! I'd beaten Bex to it. Get in there, Courtney!

QUACK-QUACK.

QUACK-QUACK.

Everyone looked around, like – *what?*

But I froze, holding my breath . . . because I knew immediately what the noise was. Lois's new phone, quacking to the world that she had a text.

A text from me.

In a lesson.

Oh no, why wasn't her phone on silent like it usually was? No one left their phone on loud at school!

I felt my whole face burn up.

Cave Woman was looking coolly along the front row. She was deaf, but not that deaf.

'Was that you, Kai?'

But Kai just swung round, and pointed at Lois. 'Her phone . . . in her bag.'

What a grossoid! He was always dobbing people in like that.

Cave Woman held out her hand to Lois.

Lois stood up. I could just see the side of her face – she'd gone bright red. She pulled her phone out of her bag, glanced down quickly at the screen, and then handed it over.

'You know the rules – confiscated until tomorrow, and a letter home to your parents,' Cave Woman said, briskly. 'Now back to it, everyone. I want at least a page from all of you by the end of the lesson.'

She looked back at her work.

Everyone went silent then, scribbling like mad.

I could see by the way Lois was sitting that she was upset. And she'd obviously seen the text was from me. I wished she'd turn around, so I could say sorry, but she didn't.

Of course Bex missed none of this. She took one look at my face and leant back in her seat.

'I reckon that text was from you, Courtney, wasn't it?' she hissed. 'Well done. That's Lois's new phone gone. She'll be so angry with you.'

She was right!

I was trying not to panic, but I could feel my face flushing. Oh, what could I do?

I'd have to confess at least . . .

I stuck my hand up.

'Miss Cave! It's not Lois's fault that her phone . . .'

'Hand down, Courtney, please.'

'But, miss . . .'

'No one should have their phone on in a lesson, and that's it. Now please get on with your work.'

I could see it was hopeless – she had one of those firm looks on her face, so I shut up.

I hoped Lois would turn round and smile at me for trying, but she was too busy dabbing her eyes with her sleeves.

Oh no . . . now she wouldn't have her new phone for her birthday evening.

Because of me . . .

She'd be so fed up. And then she probably WOULD go to the film with Bex.

I was feeling even hotter now. I held my face in my hands, trying to gulp back my tears. I felt all weak, like I could hardly stay in my chair.

My brain was gummed up, on go-slow . . . And then finally I twigged . . . the worry magic was coming! Coming to help me dream-fix this mess.

The wooziness rolled over me in big waves. I laid my head down on my table . . . and went out like a light.

In Cave Woman's lesson.

Chapter Nineteen

The dream spun in lots of colours like a kaleidoscope. All I got was glimpses . . . Miss Cave smiling. Lois holding her phone and hugging me. Bex sulking. A huge ketchuppy chip. And then the fade . . .

'Courtney . . .'

I sat up so quickly I jarred my neck.

Cave Woman was standing by my chair.

The whole class had frozen, like Cave Woman had brought on an actual mini ice age as she'd crossed the room.

'See me after the lesson,' she said, quietly.

The bell went right then, but still no one moved. I think everyone was waiting to watch Cave-Woman gnaw on my bones.

And Miss Cave definitely wasn't smiling like she was supposed to be. Maybe the dream hadn't worked!

'Papers on my desk. Everyone out now, please,' she said.

The room emptied.

Leaving me and Cave Woman alone.

I stared down at my hands.

My tummy was a hard ball, and I seemed to have forgotten how to breathe.

I really was for the high jump now . . .

Cave Woman perched on a nearby desk

'So what's going on, Courtney?' The coldness in her voice had completely gone.

I looked up in surprise.

And then she smiled.

It was only a little smile, but I swear I'd not seen her smile even once since September. I'd never even seen her teeth.

Oh, lovely magic – you DID do it!

'What happened back then?' She sounded so different. Kind, even.

'Um . . . I was just . . . er . . . tired.'

What could I say? – *'I was just having a quick magic dream in your lesson. You know, like you do.'*

I took another sneaky glance at her. She was still looking at me with gentle eyes.

I looked away quickly and blurted:

'Miss, sorry – it was my fault Lois's phone went off. I texted her.' My voice was trembling as I confessed. I HATED being in trouble. 'Please! Tell me off, not her. And write to my parents, not hers. It's her birthday, see – please can she have her phone back?'

I didn't dare look at her again. I picked at my nail while she sort of hummed and then sighed.

'Well, I'm not known for bending the rules, but I appreciate your honesty, so I'm going to let it drop this time,' she said. 'You can give Lois her phone back as it's her birthday and we'll leave it at that.'

'Really? Oh, thanks, miss!'

I couldn't believe it. She really had been magicked nicer!

'And I promise I won't . . . er . . . doze off in your lesson again.'

She nodded, looking at me hard. 'And please, Courtney, do talk to me again if you're worried about anything. Any time.'

Worried about anything?! Huh, she had no idea.

I nodded back at her.

'Erm . . . please can I go now, miss?'

She went to her desk and handed me the phone.

I beamed at her, took it, and got out the door as fast as I could.

Wow – and how cool that the magic could even crack a hard nut like Cavey! I just knew it could sort out really difficult stuff . . .

Good job too, with Mum and Dad arguing all the time.

And poor Gran . . .

I ran to the canteen to find Lois.

Chapter Twenty

Lois was standing against the radiator in the corner by herself, looking really sad.

I pushed through the lunch crowd, wondering where Bex had got to.

'I got it back!' I cried, waving her phone above my head.

'Oh, wow!' Lois's face lit up. 'HOW did you manage that?'

'Skills,' I said, winking at her.

She squealed and hugged me.

Just like my cool dream.

'Right, come on! Let's get in the lunch queue. I'm having two birthday puddings to celebrate. Maybe even three!' she said, dragging me by the hand.

'Where's Bex?' I asked. Not that I exactly cared. But she was usually hanging around.

'She had to go and see Mrs Dexham – she got in trouble in maths this morning or something.'

Good – she was out of the way for a bit then.

Lois had brightened up, chatting away all bubbly while we queued.

'So can you come to mine after school – for cake?'

When I nodded, she lowered her voice and looked around her.

'I had to ask you when Bex wasn't here, see. I can't invite her round to mine cos my family aren't keen on her. My mum says she acts too grown up for her age, and Max calls her T-Rex . . .'

I tried not to snigger.

'I tell him to shut up. He can be a bit too mean sometimes,' said Lois. 'But they love YOU, of course!' she said, prodding me. 'And maybe after, we can go for a quick swim. Do you want to? I think we're getting takeaway for tea, but apart from that we're not doing much birthday-ish stuff tonight, as it's a school day.'

'Yeah, yeah – that's cool.' I smiled. This was working out exactly as I'd hoped.

But the moment I thought that, of course Bex arrived.

She came over, but as soon as she saw Lois was with me, she got on the longest donkey face ever.

'Courts got my phone back off Cavey!' said Lois, hugging me again. 'It's a miracle!'

Bex looked like this was the worst news she'd had all year.

'Oh,' she said, flicking her hair and looking away. 'But it was still pretty stupid of you to TEXT Lois in an actual lesson, Courtney...' She wanted to keep the argument going. She wanted Lois to be angry with me so much.

'Never mind now,' said Lois. 'I got it back! And anyway, I really should've put it on silent – what a numpty.' She grinned at me.

'Yeah, but . . .' Bex started again.

'Oi, stop pushing in!' said some boys behind us in the queue to Bex. 'Go to the back!'

'Oh, get over it!' Bex made a rude sign at them, and turned to Lois.

'So you wanna meet up after school? Maybe go to the cinema?'

Lois went pink and stammered –

'Um, well . . . I've sort of planned stuff with Courts and . . . er . . . my family, but . . .'

The boys in the queue started a chant at Bex: 'BACK, BACK, BACK!'

Bex gave me a shrivelling look. And without another word, she turned away and humphed off out the dining room.

'Uh-oh again,' Lois said. 'Oh dear . . .'

'Hmmmm,' I said, biting the inside of my cheeks to stop myself grinning. I didn't want Lois to think I was being mean, but really I was so happy inside.

We got chips and chocolate pudding. Lois got TWO puddings off the dinner lady when I said it was her birthday. We sat by ourselves at the end of a table, giggling and talking in silly voices. Then she made a funny face at me as she dipped a long chip in ketchup and stuffed it in her mouth.

A extra-long, ketchuppy chip.

Exactly like in my dream.

Chapter Twenty-one

On the way back to her house after school, me and Lois stopped off at the park cafe as a treat. There was the usual group of older girls from school sitting outside, drinking Diet Cokes.

Me and Lois got enormous birthday hot choccies with flakes and whizzy cream, and sat outside too.

'And then cake at mine after – whoop!' said Lois. She was such a sugar-plum fairy – she loved sweet stuff.

It was starting to get dark, but it wasn't cold. Someone was having a bonfire somewhere and it smelt lovely and smoky. We cuddled our hot choccies and chatted on as the light faded.

Then across the dusky park I spotted a boy on a bike riding along the path towards us. A tall boy with glasses.

It really looked like Kyle.

Yep, it was definitely him – he had this funny way of riding, which made his elbows stick out. I never knew why he did that. He was just weird.

'Oh, look out – it's my brother,' I said.

But what was he doing out? He had karate tonight.

I felt a little worry niggle in my tummy. Maybe something had happened at home? I knew I should've gone straight back . . . I hadn't been worrying nearly enough.

I sighed quietly to myself.

This worry magic was so epic. But honestly, I was starting to feel that I couldn't EVER go out in case something happened that needed magicking better . . . I needed to be on worry-guard all the time.

Kyle wobbled past us.

'Kyle!' I yelled. He looked round in surprise, then did this rubbish skid and stopped. He backed his bike up.

'Hey, *Kyle*,' called out one of the older girls nearby.

He went as red as a human can ever go without actual face paint. He always did near girls these days. Such a wuss.

'Y'right,' he grunted, in a trying-to-be-cool kind of voice. Except he was panting a bit from pedalling so fast, so it came out like an odd hiccup.

Total fail.

He fidgeted with his bike handlebars, and raised his eyebrows at me, opening his mouth to say something, and then shutting it again.

'Why aren't you at karate?' I said. 'What's happened?'

He half shrugged and stared at me hard – like he was trying to mind-meld with me so he didn't have to actually speak.

The girls were sniggering now.

This was overload for Kyle. 'If you want to talk to me, you have to come,' he muttered. Then he chucked his bike around and cycled off into the middle of the footie pitch. He waved at me to go over.

Lois looked at me, and we both laughed.

Poor old Kylsie and his tomatoey face.

I staggered up, sighing. 'I s'pose I'd better go and find out what's going on.'

Kyle was riding in a slow circle, glaring over at me.

'Wait right there,' I said to Lois. 'I'll be back!'

But as I jogged over to Kyle, my heart got faster.

Please don't let it be something bad about Gran.

'What's up?' I huffed.

'Nothing,' said Kyle. I could tell he was hesitating – like he didn't want to tell me. 'Just . . .'

'Just what? Why are you out?'

He stopped by the fence.

'Mum sent me to the shop to buy stuff . . .' he sighed. 'Cos she's got Zac and Mercedes round there, instead of them going to after-school club.'

I threw my head back. 'Zac and Mercedes? No WAAAY!'

Zac and Mercedes lived six doors up with their loud mum, Lou. They were annoying times ten billion. Zac was about three and screamed all the time. Mercedes was six, as mouthy as her mum, and actually thought she was Lady Gaga. She was always doing these wiggly dances – and her mum even let her have spray tan sometimes.

I was shaking my head. 'But why?'

Kyle rolled his eyes. 'Because Mum's got it into her head that she could do some childminding to make some extra cash.'

'Childminding? What do you mean, they'd be round ours ALL the time?' I said.

'It's a nightmare already,' said Kyle, pulling his brakes on and off. 'They've wrecked the place. Mum begged me to miss karate, and sent me up to the shop for a load of biscuits to shut them up. They've already eaten all Dad's orange Club biscuits. And his diet bars.'

He rolled his bike forward and back.

'So I gotta get to the shop now,' he said. 'But it's gonna take more than biscuits to shut those two up.'

'And I'd better go straight home,' I muttered, half to myself. 'Try and tidy up or Dad'll have ten fits about the mess.' My mind was already loop-the-looping with all the trouble this would cause.

'Courtney – don't be an idiot . . . just stay out with Lois.'

'No, Kyle! WHY do you think you can tell me what to do all the time?' I walked away from him, back towards the cafe. 'I'm not five!'

'Well, suit yourself . . .' he called after me.

I heard him cycle away . . .

Good, bog off, rubbish brother . . .

But I was SO glad he had told me what was happening . . .

Except now I was going to have to tell Lois I couldn't stay out with her.

On her birthday.

Lois was still waiting for me, shivering a bit with two empty hot choc glasses in front of her. She looked at me with wide eyes as I hurried up to her.

'Is it your gran?' she asked, nervously.

'No, no . . . it's . . . um . . . complicated. But I'm SOOO sorry,' I cried, 'I just have to go. Please don't hate me. We can have our birthday swim and cake on Saturday to make up for it, yeah?'

'Yeah, yeah – no probs,' she said, sounding surprised. Then she looked down, and I could tell she was a bit upset too.

'I'm so sorry,' I said again. 'See you tomorrow.' Then I gave her a quick hug, and broke into a run across the park.

I had to get back and get tidying. And try and talk Mum out of this.

If not, I'd have to sort it out with worry magic. FAST.

Chapter Twenty-two

I nearly tripped over onto my face as I came through the door.

A big box of our old toys and games was upside down in the hall – Mum had obviously been in the attic.

The telly was blasting from the lounge. I could see Mercedes in there, prancing around to a Girls Aloud song. All arms in the air and bum-wiggles, and wearing some kind of weird, too-tight, leotard-dress thing. It was *wrong*.

There were clothes, games pieces, books,

shoes and broken biscuits all over the floor.

I stepped between things, and went straight into the lounge and switched the telly off.

Mercedes put her hands on her hips. 'Aww, why d'yer do that, *Courtney*?'

'Because it's junk,' I said, 'and it's making my ears burst.'

'Right, I'm telling!' said Mercedes. She swung her bunches at me, and pouted off to the kitchen. I could hear her whining on to Mum.

Mum came in, looking hot. Lots of her hair had frizzed out of her ponytail.

'Oh hi, Courts,' she said, wiping her arm across her forehead. 'Please could you let Mercy do her dancing, darling? Just for a bit.'

Mercedes cocked her head at me with this *ha-ha* look on her face, and put the telly back on LOUD.

'Mum!' I cried, turning the telly down again. 'But Dad'll be back soon.'

My chest went tight at the thought. Dad really wouldn't deal with this mess.

'Well, he'll have to put up with it for today,' she said, pushing her hair back, all flustered. 'He wants me to find some work, and, look – I'm *trying* . . .' Then she lowered her voice. 'And it's just a trial session, but to be honest it's not going as I hoped . . .'

You don't say, Mum . . .

Zac stomped into the room, holding a plant. He cackled like a cartoon baddie, and emptied the plant and mud all over the carpet.

I gawped. This wasn't childminding – it was evil goblin-minding.

'Oh, I'll take that, sweet pea, shall I?' said Mum, hooking the pot out of Zac's hand. 'Good boy – well done.'

She turned aside to me and whispered out of the corner of her mouth. 'They'll be gone by seven – I can't get rid of them quicker.'

'Seven?!' My heart skipped. 'But Dad will definitely be here by then!'

'I can't help that, but you just go to your room and I'll deal with them.' She shooed me towards the door. 'And don't you start *worrying*.'

DON'T worry? How was I supposed to do that?

No, I was going to worry really WELL and then the magic might come. It looked like magic might be the only way out of this trouble.

'It's fine, Mum. I'll stay and help,' I said.

The porch door opened just then and Kyle appeared in the hall. He dumped his bag of shopping on the hall table and ran straight upstairs. Really, he was like a ghost brother, melting into the walls at any sign of trouble. So feeble.

Mum just shook her head, turned back to the wrecked room and tugged her hands through her hair.

'OK, everyone – let's all tidy up together!' she cried, all brightly. 'Whoop, whoop! Best Tidier-Upper gets a sticker!'

She started moving about the room, picking things up.

'*Tidy, tidy all the toys! Put them all away . . .*' she sang to the tune of *Row Your Boat* in a new, chirrupy, playgroup voice. 'Come on, everyone! Join in with the Tidy-up Song while you work!' She was just trying way too hard.

Mercedes obviously didn't think 'everyone' meant her, and just plonked her bum down in front of the telly to watch another music video. And, as for Zac, it was like he'd heard the word TIDY but his awkward little brain had reversed it. He took a board game out of a cardboard box, and shook everything out of it, behind the sofa.

'Oh dear, dear,' said Mum weakly, sinking down onto the chair. '"Tidy" means we put things *back* in the toy box, Zackie.'

'He might do it if you give him some money,' said Mercedes, her eyes still on the telly. 'Mum gave him a two-pound coin yesterday to stop biting me, and he did.'

Oka-a-ay, so you had to PAY Zac to stop behaving like an orc.

'Oh, no!' said Mum, looking shocked. 'I'm sure Zackie would help me for this *lovely* train sticker,' she continued, picking up a sheet of stickers.

'NAAAA train! DIGGER!' he yelled. He snatched the sticker sheet out of Mum's hand and spat on it.

Mum's mouth dropped open. She looked at him like he was about to chew her head off, and there was nothing she could do about it.

Really, this was hopeless.

I looked at my watch. I needed to do something fast or the house would never get tidied.

'OK, Mum, I'll take them outside to play for ten minutes, and you clear up,' I said, firmly.

She turned to me with grateful eyes.

'Really? Oh, thanks so much, Courts, love, she said. 'I'll call Kyle down to help you, and . . .' she whispered, '*I promise they won't come again.*'

I nodded. At least she was seeing some sense.

Mum stuffed Zac and Mercedes into their coats and cooed them out of the back door. Kyle came slumping out too, wearing just short sleeves and a big scowl. He clearly didn't want to muppet-sit any more than me.

It was really quite dark out, so Mum put the garden floodlight on. I pulled my coat round myself, and watched Zac loon about, shouting at birds.

Well, THIS was fun.

'You HAVE to play with us now – your mum said,' said Mercedes, standing in the middle of the lawn with her hands on her hips. 'And I want to play Teenagers at a Party.'

Kyle sniggered and walked up the garden, shaking his head. Obviously no help at all, as usual.

'Can't we just do some drawing or something – on the picnic table?' I said. 'I'll go and get my felt tips. I've got glitter ones somewhere.'

'NO-O-O!' squeaked Mercedes. 'I want to play teenagers. Or I'm going in.'

Going In was not in my plan. The house was trashed enough already. And now Dad had put a padlock on his Shed after the whole Derek thing, there was less to mess up outside.

'OK,' I sighed. 'You start.'

And – OMG – she didn't need asking twice.

'Yeah, yeah, WHOOP WHOOP!' she sang. 'This party is well siiiick, man. And let's give a big shout-out for DJ Bants. Safe!' Her voice had gone all American, and she was doing more of those cringey bum-wriggles around the garden.

Me and Kyle stared at her.

'*Someone* watches too much telly,' said Kyle.

'You have to dance too!' she said, pointing at me. 'And you can be the DJ,' she said to Kyle.

'Great . . . enjoying this,' said Kyle. 'Looks like you're dancing, then, Courts. Do it!

I gave him a cold stare. I was not moving even a toe.

Mercedes twirled up the garden, doing weird ballet-ish pirouettes. I couldn't be sure, but I didn't really think teenagers did that, let alone at a party . . .

It was only then that I realised that Zac had gone quiet. Too quiet . . .

I spun round and there he was, ploughing his feet through Dad's veg patch – right across the neat lines of leeks, and then back again.

Noooo! Trust him to find something to mess up.

'NO, Zac! Get off there,' I yelled, running over.

'Vroooooooooom,' he yelled, throwing me a toothy grin. Vrooooom-vroooom all through Dad's artichokes.

'And Zackie can be the DJ's big, yellow digger,' sang Mercedes, her bunches bouncing wildly.

I caught Zac's hood, but he yanked away from me, and fell flat on his back, breaking off two of Dad's broccoli plants.

'WAAAAAAAA,' he wailed, getting up and waddle-running towards the house. 'I want my mummy. And I need a pee pee . . .'

Mercedes stopped dancing for a second.

'He waves his widdle around if he goes by himself,' she said, cheerfully, 'and the pee splashes on the walls.'

Zac was holding onto his trousers and hopping from foot to foot at the back door.

'You go after him,' I said to Kyle. This was *definitely* a boy's job.

Kyle made a face, but bounded over and took Zac in.

I sat on the bench and watched Mercedes' strange dancing-and-singing show. Her singing got louder and more out of tune, and then she moved onto wonky handstands with wildly kicking legs.

Brrr, it was freezing . . .

I hoped Mum was hurrying up with the tidying and doing a good job. Dad didn't rate her as a tidier – she hated housework.

Zac came waddling back out of the house just then, with his trousers half pulled up.

All by himself.

No sign of Kyle-the-babysitter.

And as he trip-trotted across the lawn, I looked closer . . . and my heart nearly stopped.

Zac was holding Henners.

Dad's darlingest little Henners.

No! He must have got him out of his bathroom cage!

KYLE! So useless!

I jumped to my feet.

'Mercy! Look at my Mickley Mouse,' Zac lisped, gripping Henners so tight I was sure his ratty eyes were popping out. But Mercedes was too busy in her World of Stupid Handstands to listen.

'ZAC, be gentle! Stand still!' I ordered, walking towards him slowly in case he threw a wobbler and dropped Henners on his head.

Kyle appeared in the doorway. He took one look at Zac and Henners, and went white. He knew he'd messed up big time. The babysitting fail of the year.

'Oh, well done . . .' I began, looking at him all daggers. But I stopped mid-sentence.

Because right behind Kyle was Dad.

Chapter Twenty-three

Dad clocked everything in two seconds flat. His eyebrows went into one long, angry caterpillar, and he made a squawky noise.

'He's got Henners!' he yelled.

He started bounding over.

'It's OK, Dad!' I cried. 'I'll catch him!' I lunged at Zac, my heart booming in my head. I caught Zac's sleeve, but he tugged away from me.

'No, I wanna show Mercy my mousey!' Zac cried, scooting past me towards his sister.

Mercedes had her back to us, lost in a frenzy of handstands. She was counting each time she flipped her legs up . . .

'59, 60, 61, 62 . . .'

Zac shoved Henners right in her face just when she was upside down for number 63.

Of course, she screamed, and tumbled down in a big pile.

Landing right on top of Henners, squashing him flat.

Poor Henners! He staggered out from under Mercedes, making small, sad squeaks. Dad tried to nab him, but somehow Henners slunk through his fingers and hobbled under the holly bush in the flowerbed.

Me, Dad and Kyle all got down on our knees to peer under the bush, but it was so thick and dark we couldn't see a thing.

'Was he limping? He was, wasn't he?' growled Dad, lying flat on his tummy to get a better look. 'He'd better not be hurt!'

Then Mum came flying across the lawn.

'Oh, what's happened?' she cried.

Dad knelt up and narrowed his eyes at her.

'YOU let that child play with Henners, that's what!' He fired his words out like cold bullets.

'No, I never did!' yelped Mum. 'I DID NOT!' Oh no, and they were off . . .

My tummy lurched, and panic zinged through me. My throat suddenly felt like it was sealing up and I had to pant some deep breaths.

What if Henners was really hurt – and all because of Mum and her rubbish childminding? Dad was going to go bonkers-berserk at her . . .

Ooh, my blood was rushing through my head, and I felt cold and hot at the same time.

'Hen-n-n-ers . . .' I called. My voice sounded stuttery and odd.

I was still on all fours on the lawn, but I felt myself suddenly sway. My legs and arms buckled under me, and I pancaked down – splat – onto the wet ground.

I tasted mud as my eyes closed.

Chapter Twenty-four

It was the shortest dream – with melting colours and just little peeks at things: moon faces. Mum and Dad talking calmly. Henners scampering, and then sitting on his back legs, lit up, and glowing bright white in the darkness. Mercedes and Zac going out of the door with flashing torches . . .

As I came to, I could hear Mercedes and Zac shrieking excitedly as if Christmas had suddenly come.

'Cwourtney got deaded!' yelled Zac, skipping around me.

I flicked open my eyes and looked up. Three pale faces. Like moons against the sky in the floodlight.

Mum, Dad, Kyle.

Moon faces . . .

I pulled myself up on my elbows. But had the rest of the dream come true? Please, magic – work, work!

'There you go now,' Dad pulled me gently to my feet, but kept hold of my arms. 'You're OK.'

'Courts?' whispered Mum, her voice wavering.

'Yeah, I'm completely fine, Mum,' I said, brushing mud off my hands.

Mum hugged me to her, but I could tell she was mouthing something to Dad over my head, and then he mouthed some stuff back. I couldn't catch what they were saying, but – hey – at least they were calm. Another point to the magic!

'Right,' said Dad in his bossiest voice. 'Kyle, please stay out here to look for Henners. He'll be in the garden somewhere.'

Kyle looked ahead with blank eyes, like he wanted to say *yes sir, no sir* again, but didn't dare.

'And you, young lady,' Dad said to me. 'Fireman's lift to the sofa – hop on.' And he grabbed me, swung me up over his shoulder, and carried me towards the house.

'Awww, I wanna carry!' whined Mercedes, running alongside us. 'Can I have a go?'

'Now, Mercy and Zac,' said Mum, very firmly, guiding Zac towards the back door too. 'We're going to meet your mummy at her work. I'm going to phone her right now . . . exciting!'

'Yay, Mummy!' cried Mercedes.

'Naa,' yelled Zac, dropping to his knees onto the patio.

'But, Zackie, you can use the special torch from the toy box to walk through the dark. It makes red AND blue light,' said Mum. Ah, she was learning . . .

Zac put his head on one side. Then he jumped up and jogged on the spot. 'Ya, ya, ya!'

Phew!

Dad plonked me down on the sofa, covered me up, and rushed out again to help hunt for Henners. I wanted to help too, but I knew they wouldn't let me.

So I lay there watching Mum phoning Lou, and then rummaging in the cardboard box in the hall for the torch and batteries with Zac and Mercedes.

Mum cooed around me a bit.

And then they left.

OMG, they actually LEFT. I could see the torch flashing as they went down the path in the dark.

More gold stars for the worry magic.

I stayed in the lounge by myself, tickling my nose with the end of my plait and worrying like mad about Henner's leg. Oh please make it OK! I'd seen him scampering in my dream, so surely his leg wasn't broken. And I'd dreamt him glowing white, like a light was shining on him in the dark – so that must mean they'd find him with their phone lights. The magic had fixed all my other worries, so it would sort this too. It would.

But Dad was ages.

And ages.

I got up and went to the back door. Dad and Kyle were coming through the gate.

'Were you looking for him out in the *street*?' I gasped. I was sure Henners wouldn't have climbed over our high fences . . .

Kyle just grimaced, and pushed past me into the house.

'There's a hole over by the fence,' said Dad. 'Kyle saw him run through it full tilt, so his leg isn't busted, at least. But we've looked all up the street, and there's no sign of him.'

I gulped, suddenly remembering something. Oh no – Henners must have got through the hole that Derek dug!

I bit my lip.

No way was I telling Dad that, though.

'God knows how the darn hole got there. Must be foxes . . . Or maybe a *dog*?' finished Dad, darkly.

Uh oh.

'Definitely foxes . . . or maybe rabbits,' I said, quickly. 'And I expect Henners'll come home soon – for some nosh.' Of course he would. Henners loved his food – he was a total pig face.

Dad nodded, but he just kept on standing

there in the doorway not coming in, with his shoulders all hunched up.

Oh poor Dad . . .

I leant my head on his arm, tears in my eyes. He let me stay there for a moment. But then he pulled away, his face twitching.

'Yeah . . . well . . . I'm sure he'll show up,' he said in a claggy voice. 'Come on – don't you start fretting again.'

He bustled me inside, grabbed a beer, and we sat in front of the telly, which was on some programme about cars. But I could see Dad wasn't really watching. And he kept rubbing his tummy, like he always does when he's upset.

Oh, it had all gone so wrong. And it was my fault! The worry magic had fixed everything I'd worried about – even Henners' leg. But I'd FORGOTTEN to worry about Derek's big hole. How could I have been so dim? I hadn't worried *properly* enough.

Mum came back in the front door, just then.

My tummy fluttered. Was Dad going to start yelling about the hole?

But he just got to his feet again.

'Going to nip out with some raisins,' he said, quietly. 'Maybe Henns will've had second thoughts about his Great Escape by now.'

Mum just nodded. Calmly. Without nagging at him or anything.

I was a bit amazed.

They were both still being nice. But the magic probably hadn't worn off yet.

'I'll help you look, Dad!' I said, hopping up.

'Oh no you don't – bed for you,' said Mum.

Dad nodded. So I went to my room, but I didn't get my PJs on. I wiped my misted-up window and squinted out into the dark. I could see Dad's shadow, and the light on his phone moving along the street as he looked under bushes. Then a cat darted across the road. Was that naughty Puddy-cat?

Oh Henners, run away fast from all those cats out there!

I threw myself down onto my bed.

I needed to worry really *thoroughly* this time, so if the magic came it would fix *everything*.

And I'd had an idea . . .

I reckoned I'd worry much better if I WROTE my worries down in a list. That way I could make sure I didn't miss any out. Yeah, it could be like playing Worry Wig, but on paper – I just had too many worries to keep track of now. And maybe I could keep the paper inside the Worry Wig?

No, there was a better place for the list . . .

I found the Worry Wig under my pillow and pulled it on, like I used to with Gran. Then I grabbed a felt tip, got my letter to Gran out of its envelope, and wrote on the back of the letter –

WORRY WIG LIST
I'm worried that a cat will catch Henners.
  Or a dog. Or a fox. Or a badger.
Or he'll get run over.
Or get lost and end up miles away and
  never find his way back.

Er . . . I chewed the end of my pen. What else? I had to think of everything that could go wrong. I couldn't forget anything or the worry magic would forget it too – and a bad thing might happen.

And I'm worried Henners'll get locked in
someone's shed.
Or someone else will catch him and keep
him as their pet.

Then I wrote 'marmite crisps flavour' next to that worry, and 'custard cream flavour' next to another one. But the joke didn't make me smile when it was me cracking it rather than Gran. It just didn't work without her there to pretend to eat them up.

I pulled the Worry Wig off cos it was making my head too hot and itchy, and immediately heard Dad's cough downstairs.

I hopped straight out onto the landing.

Dad was in the hall, taking his coat off. He looked up and spotted me at the top of the stairs . . .

'No luck yet – but you get off to bed now,' he called up.

'But did you beam your light right under all the bushes?' I asked. Why wasn't the part of my dream about Henners glowing in a beam of light coming true?

'Yes, everywhere. But don't you worry. He'll be back for breakfast – it's fine.' He was using that fake, bright voice people use to calm small children. I knew it so wasn't fine.

But I scuttled back to bed, trying not to cry, and carried on with my Worry Wig List.

*And I'm worried that Henners will fall
    down a drain hole.
Or he'll get freezing cold and get ratty flu,
    out in the street all by himself . . .*

I hoped I hadn't left anything unworried about, but I really couldn't think of anything else.

All I needed now was for the magic to come and get Henners back.

I lay there, screwing up my face, trying to force the special, panicky, spinning feeling to come on. But really, I knew it wouldn't work.

I'd tried before, and I couldn't MAKE the magic happen.

I sighed. The magic obviously didn't want to help me find Henners. I knew I hadn't worried very well, but it could still help me now. Why was it keeping away?

Well, I'd have to go out and look for Henners myself then.

I snatched the old Winnie the Pooh torch that used to be Kyle's from my bedside drawer, and slid downstairs. Mum was in their room, and Dad was in the lounge, so I got out to the back without anyone bossing me back upstairs.

I pulled on my wellies and old coat and nipped out.

The street was quiet – just the odd car and dog-walker. I walked bent over, shining the torch as far as I could under all the hedges, just hoping I would spot a flash of white in the beam. I tramped along right to the end of our road, calling Henners again and again. Which was stupid, seeing as he was a rat and not a dog, and didn't even know his dumb name.

But there wasn't a ratty tail in sight.

I'd got to the crossroad near the pool. I was about to turn back when suddenly I heard a voice I knew.

Lois?

And then a loud, shrieky laugh.

Bex?

I stepped behind the bus shelter to hide, and watched them walk away up the opposite street, arm in arm. They had their backs to me, but I saw that Lois had her lemon-jelly swimming bag over her shoulder.

No way. Lois had gone swimming on her birthday after all.

But with Bex instead of ME.

Chapter Twenty-five

I went home, flew straight upstairs, got right underneath my covers, turned off my light, and cried and cried *again*.

I just COULD NOT believe that Lois had done this. I knew I'd ditched her at the last minute. But why did she have to invite Bex to go *swimming*? It was OUR special thing. Just ours. And now Bex would probably want to come each time.

I wiped my eyes on my Worry Wig.

And what if Lois had a better time swimming with Bex? Maybe they'd both got *stupid* matching bikinis to go with their *stupid* matching lip balm.

GRRRRRRRRRRRRR!

I lay there, wide awake, for ages.

Puddy came and lay right on my tummy, blinking at me and padding the covers with fat happy paws. He was too heavy, but I let him stay there.

'Oh, Puddy, at least *you're* my friend, aren't you?' I whispered, kissing his head.

Mum crept in to say goodnight, and I just yawned like I was sleepy. But I wasn't. All my worries were churning like my head was a washing machine. I couldn't stop thinking about everything over and over. Henners, Lois, Bex, Mum and Dad, Gran . . . and the magic not coming.

I sat up and put my light on. I found Gran's letter and added to my Worry Wig List –

I'm worried that Lois secretly wants to be best friends with Bex instead of me. And I'm worried that my worry magic has all run out, and won't come to fix stuff any more.

I dropped the letter into my drawer, and turned my light off again.

But I was squirming, turning and waking up all night long.

In the morning, it was a school day, but I didn't get dressed. I went straight down to check Henners' cage in my nightclothes.

The cage door was still swinging open.

He wasn't back.

Dad had already gone to work, and Mum and Kyle were all long-faced and quiet.

I felt sick, I was worrying so much. How could I go to school when Henners was *lost*, maybe forever? I wouldn't be able to concentrate. And I needed to be at home so I could be ready to worry-magic things better – IF the magic ever decided to come again. I didn't want anything *else* to go wrong.

And I'd see Lois and Bex at school too. I just knew Bex would just go on and on about how fun swimming had been – she was going to be SO cowbag-annoying about it. *And* I was worried that if I saw Lois, I might say something cross to her, and then she definitely WOULD like Bex more.

So I waited until Kyle went upstairs. Then I started acting up.

'Ow, Mum, my tummy really hurts. I don't feel very well.'

I sagged down on the kitchen stool and looked at her with big eyes. Performance of my life.

'Oh dear, maybe you've got a bug,' said Mum, feeling my forehead. 'Or are you anxious about Gran again?'

I started to nod.

'Yes . . . Dad and I were saying last night that if this continues we really should get Dr Prop to refer you to a paediatrician.'

I stopped nodding.

'No, it's probably just a little tummy bug,' I said, quickly.

Mum stroked my face. 'OK – maybe a day of quiet resting would do you good. You get back into bed. I'll ring the sanctuary and tell them I can only come in for an hour this morning.'

So I went back to my room. Kyle walked past my door and looked in at me, still in my PJs.

'You skiving off?' he said.

'I'm ill – bad tummy.'

He gave me a look like he didn't believe me at all.

But Mum looked after me loads. She brought me ginger ale and dry toast for my tummy. I was really hungry, but I had to pretend I was too ill to eat in case she got suspicious.

I heard her on the phone in the hall once, and I crept onto the landing to have a sly listen. I just needed to check she wasn't cooking up any more plans that would wind Dad up. But it was only her friend, Linze.

Then, as soon as she left for the sanctuary, I hopped straight downstairs. I scoffed down one of Dad's homemade Smarties cookies. Then I put my wellies on and hunted all around the garden for Henners again. No luck . . .

I wanted to look out in the street too, but I didn't dare in case someone saw me and sent one of those truant-police people round to arrest me.

I went back in, but I felt strange and restless. The house was looking really jumble-saley *again*, so I passed the time by tidying up and straightening stuff. I hoped it'd help get Dad a bit happier, at least.

I even sorted out his spice rack. Mum had put the jars back wonky, and she'd left a few lids half on – and I knew Dad'd grumble like mad next time he was making one of his curries. So I wiped each jar and put them all back in alphabetical order. There . . . good. All tidy for him now.

Then I went and sat on the loo next to Henners' cage. Someone had left the bathroom window open – maybe Dad had done it, hoping Henners might come home by himself. But how would we ever know if he did? He might be a naughty rat and sneak in, eat his raisins and then hip-hop out again.

Then I remembered something I'd seen on a detective programme on the telly once.

Yes!

I got some flour and sprinkled it on the windowsill and on the floor in front of his cage – along with a pile of raisins next to his cosy bed to tempt him in. Now we'd be able to see his little pawprints in the flour if he came in.

Ha . . .

And then we'd know he was still alive . . .

Ugh – my tummy turned. Please stay alive, Henners.

And Gran . . .

I shuddered, and hurried away from those nasty thoughts into the kitchen. I grabbed a four-pack of Dad's diet chocolate mousses, and went to my room to watch any old telly – CBeebies and any baby stuff as long as it was happy and bright. I gulped down three of the mousses and hid the pots at the bottom of my bin.

Then I actually felt sick – for real.

Mum came back. She popped up to check on me, but I pretended to be asleep. Then when she'd gone, I whipped out onto the landing again to listen to what she was doing. Just in case she'd brought a monkey or maybe some actual *elephants* back from the sanctuary, or some other duh-ness that needed worrying about. But I could hear she was just washing up, all innocent.

I hopped back to bed. It was weird really. Mum thought she was staying home to check on me. But she didn't realise I was checking up on her too!

It was a long day.

The rain pattered at the windows. I flumped out on my bed, messing with the Worry Wig, twisting all its fur and giving it spiky hair-dos, as my mind fretted over stuff.

Puddy-cat stretched out next to me, upside down and fast asleep.

I knew how he felt. Just so done in and exhausted.

Worrying was hard work – there was so much that could go wrong all the time, and I had to think of everything.

All my fiddling had made the Worry Wig matted. I tried to comb through the knots with my fingers, but the fur was way too tangled up.

I threw it down on my bed, and went downstairs to get some water and check the flour. No pawprints.

I let Mum make me more dry toast, and slept in a heap on the sofa in front of the fire.

After school-time I got a text from Lois.

Hope ur feeling better, babes? xx

But I didn't reply.

Chapter Twenty-six

The day got even *worse* later.

I heard Dad come in the front door. But instead of trudging down the hall to the kitchen as usual, he just pegged it straight upstairs . . . actually ran . . . and then clicked their bedroom door shut behind him.

It was totally un-Dad-ish.

Was he that upset about Henners?

Or was it Gran?

Prickles ran all up me.

Oh no . . .

I crept up the stairs in my socks, and listened outside the door. Of course I knew I shouldn't, but I did anyway.

I could hear the bed creaking. And Dad . . . sniffing.

Sniffing?

Was he *crying?*

Maybe something *really* bad had happened . . .

I got goosebumps.

'Dad?' I called, totally forgetting I wasn't supposed to be there, nosing.

My heart was beating loud in my ears while I waited.

Silence.

Slowly I pushed down the door handle and opened the door just a sliver.

'Who's that?' Dad sounded startled – as if he hadn't heard me before.

I shut the door quickly, but not before I'd seen him. Lying under the covers, his face all red and crumpled up.

He WAS crying.

I caught my breath.

I leant my forehead against the wall, and knocked softly.

'Dad, what's wrong? Is Gran all right?' I called though the door.

I waited, holding my breath so I could listen inside the room.

'She had a bad day today, but yes, she's all right,' he croaked, finally.

That didn't sound good. Not good at all.

'So she's OK?'

Another long pause. A sob began bulging in my throat, making it ache. I scuffled my feet against the door.

'Yes.' His voice sounded odd. 'She's in the best place – your gran's going to be just fine.'

Fine. Except he was crying, and he NEVER cried.

I went back to my room, but I felt too fidgety. So I huddled in my doorway, hugging my knees, my eyes dribbling tears, just waiting for Dad to come out.

I didn't have to wait long. Their bedroom door suddenly scraped open, and Dad came muscle-manning out. He didn't notice me sitting there. But my mouth dropped open.

In his hand was a huge bin liner. He'd found the squeezy roast-chicken toys!

BUT HOW?

He stood at the top of the stairs, and yelled down.

'Donna! WHAT on earth are these?'

I heard Mum's footsteps coming out of the kitchen.

'They're from a car boot sale,' said Mum, her voice snappy. 'Just second-hand dog toys I got cheap. Where did you find them? I've been looking for those.'

I could only see one side of Dad's face. He still looked creased and red, but an angry red now, and his tears had dried up. Mum would never guess he'd been crying three minutes before.

He made a furious, gritted-teeth noise.

'So clearly I was talking to myself the other night, then.' His voice was getting louder. 'Did you not hear when I said we can't afford to go shopping?!'

'Andy – they only cost £10! Stop being so unreasonable. I'm saving them as presents for any dogs at the sanctuary over Christmas.'

'So now I'm doggy Santa Claus, am I?' Dad snarled. And he upended the bin liner and shook it. All the rubbery chickens came bouncing out, and *doing-doing*ed down the stairs. It should have been a bit funny, but actually it felt more like a nightmare cartoon. One chicken fell at Dad's feet and he kicked it away like it might give him a disease.

I'd already been upset, but now tears were flooding out of me. But Dad still hadn't noticed me sitting in my doorway behind him.

Mum was shrieking from the hall. 'How DARE you behave like that!' Then she swore, and I heard her slam the kitchen door.

'You live in cloud cuckoo land,' yelled Dad, crashing down the stairs. 'I may as well talk to a wall . . . I've had enough . . . ENOUGH!'

Enough?

But what did that mean?

I could hear them in the kitchen, bawling. I

was trembling and my throat felt strangled. I bit my dressing gown sleeve hard, and pressed my eyeballs with my fingers.

Oh no, this was worse than ever.

I held my head in my hands.

And then Kyle's legs appeared in front of me. And without saying a single word, he shoved me so hard I sort of roly-polied back into my bedroom and one of my slippers came off. He closed my door and I heard the key turn on the outside.

He'd LOCKED me in!

What *the* . . . ?! But WHY?

I leapt up and pummelled the door, my head whirling dizzily.

'Kyle, you idiot! Let me out NOW!'

I kept yelling, but he didn't come. And Mum and Dad couldn't hear me cos they were too busy doing their own shouting in the kitchen.

I swallowed down my tears, and kept calling and knocking. Still no one came.

I sank to my knees with a whimper.

Oh, why did Dad have to find that shopping, just when he was so upset about Gran?

What would happen now? And what did Dad mean by 'I've had enough'? Would he stalk out again, and go wherever he kept going all the time?

To borrow another girlie tissue?

My whole body was trembling. My head spun and my brain was fuzzy.

Then I clicked . . . Oh, the magic – it was coming back again!

I lay down on my carpet with my head jammed up against my door.

And zonked out.

Chapter Twenty-seven

The dream was perfect, as usual. The roast chickens were all tidied up back into a bag. Dad and Mum both had calm, nice faces. And then – random! – a big bag of my favourite toffee popcorn.

I woke up with a start. The carpet was itching my wet cheek.

I knelt up and tugged at my door handle, but it was still locked.

'KYLE!' I yelled again. 'Let me out . . .'

I listened. No one was coming, but I could hear

Mum ranting on downstairs at top volume. And then Dad shouting back.

My heart skipped.

What? They were supposed to be *calm* now. Had the dream magic not WORKED?

'KYLE!' I hollered even louder.

And this time I heard soft footsteps and the key turning. I flung the door open, pushed past Kyle and looked over the banister.

OH NO . . . ! The hall was *still* covered with dumb rubber roast chickens. And Mum and Dad were *still* having a full-on battle in the kitchen . . .

The magic definitely HADN'T worked.

And I thought I knew why.

Because stupid, STUPID Kyle had locked me away in my room, and the magic couldn't work by remote control.

Arggh, Kyle!

Livid, I whipped round at him, but he'd disappeared.

'Courtney – get in here!' he called from his room, chilled as anything.

Well, he wouldn't be chilled when I'd finished with him! I stamped in there, pushing his door hard so it cracked against the wall.

I hadn't been in his room for ages – it smelt like old pizza, and his carpet was covered with dirty clothes.

He was sitting at his desk with his hands behind his head.

'WHY . . . ? Why did you DO it?' I was shaking with crossness. 'You're such a TOTAL idiot!'

'I did it on purpose to keep you away from them,' he said, flatly. He picked up his elastic-band ball, threw it in the air and caught it. 'To stop you trying to sort them out and stressing.'

'WHAT? How COULD you?' I was nearly speechless. 'Why?'

He rolled his eyes up to the ceiling.

'Because it's so pointless . . . and you're going *mad*, Courtney! Like *totally* round the BEND!' He threw the elastic-band ball hard at the wall.

'NO I'M NOT!' I shrieked. 'At least I'm *trying* to help. And it's all right for you – you don't CARE about anyone, Mr Google Geek. You're like . . . you're like . . . Tin Man in *The Wizard of Oz*! No heart!' I bumped down onto my bum, tears starting again, choking me.

I expected him to sneer at the mention of *The Wizard of Oz* . . . like, *you baby!* – but he didn't. He just went bright red.

'Oh yes, that's right,' he hissed. 'I don't *care* when they scream at each other. I don't *care* that Gran's ill. I don't *care* that Dad NEVER ever comes to watch me play footie any more . . .' His nose wrinkled up. Like I remembered it used to when he was young and trying not to cry. I hadn't seen his nose do that for a long time.

It shut me up for a minute – I just stared at him. But then he started being super-annoying again.

'Yeah, so call me Mr Tin Man, because I don't swoon like a princess,' he muttered, his face in a huge, screwed-up frown. 'Hey, maybe I should try throwing some drama-queen hissy fits too!' He slumped forward in a pretend faint on his chair. 'Unless you're *pretending* to faint, are you?'

'Uh? I CAN'T believe you just said that!' I pushed over his pile of computer magazines next to me so they skidded all over his floor. 'Of course I'm not *pretending*,' I said, gulping down a big sob.

'Yeah, well . . .' he muttered. 'I actually believe that. No one's that good an actor, even you. So it looks like you ARE just going mad, then . . .'

Tears were filling my eyes so I couldn't even see.

I wasn't going mad. *Was I?*

'*Why* are you being so mean to me?' I whimpered.

He looked away.

'Actually I'm trying to help you. I'm –'

But he stopped as the front door slammed so hard below that the walls seemed to shake. I leapt up and ran over to his window, pulling back his silly Man U curtain.

Dad was marching off down the path. When he got under the street light, I could see him clearly. He had no coat on and . . . I rubbed the misty window to see better . . . red shoes on? No . . . his slippers.

He was leaving in his slippers? But where was he *going*? I didn't want to think about it . . .

Oh, it was all so messed-up – and I could've magicked this better, if it hadn't been for KYLE!

I slapped the tears off my face, and flew round, furious.

'Dad's stropped off! And it's all YOUR fault for locking me in. I could've stopped this . . . !'

Kyle just gave this huge sigh, and shook his head, like: *Oh dear – poor, little, confused Courtney.*

Then I'd had completely enough of Mr Smug Face.

My eyes blurred, and I bit my teeth together. I felt like all my blood was pumping through my brain. I'd not been that cross for a long time.

'GRRRRR! You are so annoying!' I shrieked. I was opening and closing my hands into tight fists. 'You think you know everything but you don't!'

And then I just started blurting – I couldn't help myself . . .

'Because by the way, I don't faint – I fall asleep and *dream*. And I dream everything better – all the things I've worried about! Really, I DO! I magic Mum and Dad nicer – like I put a spell on them and stop their fighting! And when I wake up, it's come true.'

Even as everything was spilling out of my mouth, I knew it was stupid. He was going to pooh-pooh it completely. 'It's really and truly . . . *magic*,' I finished in a whisper, lamely. 'It is . . .'

I was breathing hard. And I didn't dare look right at him, but out of the corner of my eye, I saw him wince and tug his hands through his hair.

'So let me get this straight,' he said in an *I'm-talking-to-a-stupid-person* voice. 'You actually think that you have magic dreams that CONTROL Mum and Dad and make them stop fighting?'

I nodded hard. 'Yep. But I don't *think* I do . . . I *know* I do.'

He picked up a pencil and started drumming it on his desk, chewing his cheek. Like he was trying to find a way to explain stuff to me – dummy me – in simple words.

'Courtney, things change for a short while after your fainting attacks because Mum and Dad put a lid on their fighting to calm you! But only until the next bust-up. That's all that happens.'

I stared at him, my lips trembling. WHAT?! Was that true?

'But . . . but . . .' I stammered. 'But then why did the dreams work on Lois AND Miss Cave too? They didn't even *know* about my attacks!'

But, as I said it, my stomach suddenly rolled. They didn't, *did they*? 'Yes, they know,' he said, quietly, looking right at me. 'Mum told Lois's mum and the school – I heard her tell Dad. I looked at Kyle like he'd just jumped – boo! – out of my cupboard.

I felt like the walls were wobbling. What did this mean? Had Lois been fine about the Frube thing because she was trying not to stress me out? And did Cave Woman let me off because she wanted to keep me calm?

I gulped . . .

And if Kyle was right, then had Mum and Dad carried on fighting that last time, because they didn't KNOW I'd fainted? I'd been out of sight, locked in my room . . .

So was the magic really not *real*?

It was all too much to get my head around.

I knew my mouth was open like a big O.

But then, hang on . . . *hang on* . . .

'No . . . NO! it has to be magic cos I dream about random details that come true,' I spluttered. 'Like I dreamt that Dad watched *You've Been Framed!* with me. And when I woke up, that exact same thing happened.'

Kyle pressed his lips together and swung back on his chair. 'Just chance. *You've Been framed!* repeats are on all day long!'

'No, but it happens every time!' I squeaked, stamping my foot. 'Like I dreamt we'd have takeaway pizza for tea – sweetcorn and pepperoni – and then we did! I dreamt Zac and Mercy went home with a torch – and then they did. There's always one little thing that comes true each time that no one could ever . . . er . . . *predict*. It can only be magic!'

'Coincidences,' he said, brushing the air with his hand. 'Or you're just imagining it.'

'But why would I *imagine* it?' I cried. Without a

word, he swivelled round on his chair and started tapping on his open laptop. I lay back, flat out on his carpet, and glowered at the ceiling.

I wondered what he'd put into his Google search. Probably *What to do with ridiculous fainting sisters who think they're magic?*

'There you go,' he said, tapping his screen, nodding happily. 'Dr Kyle diagnoses panic-related hallucinations. It says here that they can happen as the result of an overactive imagination, induced by stress.'

OMG, sometimes I hated my brother. Him and his show-offy geek talk. Why did he have to sound like he was forty-two instead of nearly fifteen?

'No!' I cried. 'YOU just have NO imagination! And you're not a doctor!'

He sighed, pushed his glasses up onto his forehead and rubbed his eyes. Like he was SOOO tired of my nonsense, but trying to baby me along.

I pouted back at him. I knew I probably looked like a stroppy toddler.

'The magic *is* real,' I said, under my breath again. 'You just don't understand.' And I knew it was – all those little things that came true after each dream. But I also knew Kyle was never going to believe me. Not ever.

'Courts,' he said in a weary way. 'Come on – you know *magic* doesn't exist.' He said it like the word tasted bad.

'Yes it does, Tin Man!' I spat.

'For God's sake, you do not live inside a Harry Potter book!' he sniped. 'Grow up!'

'What? ARGGGHH, I HATE YOU . . .' I swept his globe off his shelf with my foot and it went crashing into the radiator.

'Get your bum out of my room then, *Hermione*!' he roared. 'Go and be MAD somewhere else.'

I jumped up.

Kyle was just a horrible, boring know-it-all. And he was WRONG about the worry magic.

Wasn't he?

I marched to the door, kicking over his bin as I passed. Some old bits of popcorn flew out across the floor.

Popcorn? I stopped for a second. Like in my dream?

But then I saw the packet in the bin.

It wasn't my favourite toffee flavour, but SALTED popcorn. YUCK! My absolute worst kind.

The magic hadn't worked at all. Not one bit.

I stamped on the popcorn so it mashed into the carpet, and BANGED his bedroom door shut.

Chapter Twenty-eight

By half seven, Dad hadn't come home. He was still out somewhere in his silly slippers.

I looked out of my window to see if his Shed light was on, but it was totally pitch black in there. So I sent him a text asking him where he was, but he didn't answer, and when I went down for tea, his mobile was on the side in the kitchen.

Mum had made jacket potatoes and beans. Kyle was out at his computery friend Chris's, so he'd eaten his tea early. Dad's potato was sitting waiting for him by the microwave looking wrinkled up and sad.

After I checked the flour on the loo windowsill for Henners' pawprints – nothing there at all – me and Mum took our dinners on trays into the lounge. We only seemed to have telly dinners these days.

'Is Dad coming back soon, Mum?' I asked quietly.

'Oh, don't worry about him,' she said with a sharp face. 'He's probably at the pub.'

I just nodded, blew on my potato and stared at the telly.

But I KNEW that wasn't true

Number one, Dad hardly ever went to the pub – he said pints were way too expensive. And number two – Dad might not care what he looked like, but even *he* wouldn't go to the pub in his slippers.

No, he must've gone to someone's house . . . Maybe to watch the weather report . . . all evening.

My tummy did a tumble like I'd gone over a bumpy bridge.

But of course I didn't say any of that to Mum. I just kept on shovelling in my beans.

We'd just put down our knives and forks when the phone went. My heart did a little jog, but it was only one of Mum's sanctuary friends. So while she chatted on, I washed up our plates, went to my room, got into bed and worried, scribbling it all down onto my Worry Wig List for Gran. I'd nearly filled the whole page, so I wrote in small writing –

Now I'm worried Dad has a secret girlfriend. (sicky quiche flavour)
I'm worried he'll leave Mum, and I'll have to go and stay with Dad and his girlfriend at weekends. And she'll probably be mean to me like stepmums are in books. (mouldy swede flavour)

Gran usually chose nice flavours, but I knew there was no way that THOSE worries would taste nice.

Puddy came trotting in. His tail whipped up like a flag when he saw me. He sprang up on the bed with a pleased miaowy hello, and walked all over my letter, doing his extra-loud, *pring-pring* purr.

'Oh, furry-purry Pudds,' I whispered, stroking him. His fur was cold and damp, and smelt a tiny bit of car oil. 'You don't ever get worried, do you? Lucky you.'

I sighed. Worrying was actually doing my head in. Especially now, on top of everything, I was getting more and more worried about why the worry magic wasn't working properly any more. It hadn't got Henners back. And there I was half inside-out with worrying about Dad. *WHY* wasn't it helping?

My annoying brain was whispering even worse things too – like, was Kyle actually really right? Was the magic not *real*? He'd really muddled me, saying all that stuff he'd said . . . My head was getting in a right old tangle, like the Worry Wig's fur.

And if it was true that I didn't have real magic, then I wouldn't be able to fix Mum and Dad, or cure Gran . . . What would *happen*?

Argghhhhhhhh.

I quickly folded the letter away and flicked on my telly. I roamed through loads of channels, trying to find something to take my mind off things. But there was nothing good on, and I had one ear out for Dad the whole time.

He still wasn't back at bedtime.

I heard Mum coming up the stairs to say goodnight. I wanted to ask her where Dad was . . . but then again, I didn't want HER to start thinking about it too much in case she wondered if Dad had a girlfriend too. So I snapped out my light like I'd dropped off already.

But of course there was no way I could sleep.

Ten o'clock.

Half ten.

Oh, Dad . . . *where* ARE you?

I heard Mum go to bed and still I lay looking at my ceiling, just watching car headlights swoop across my room.

I got up and looked outside. It was raining.

Dad's slippers would be pretty soggy by now. They were his new ones Gran had given him.

I shivered. Oh, Gran . . .

But then . . .
Wait a minute!
My brain turned on.
Gran . . . GRAN!
OMG.
Suddenly I knew what I had to do.

Chapter Twenty-nine

I scrambled out of bed and slipped downstairs without putting the landing light on, so I didn't wake Mum.

I took Gran's spare door key with its wooden apple keyring off the hall hooks, yanked my school coat on over my onesie, and stuffed my feet into my too-small Crocs.

Then I stepped outside into the quiet, trying not to be scared. I'd never been out this late by myself before. No one was about, and the air smelt like night-time, bonfires and mud. The rain had stopped and just a silver curl of the moon was peeping from behind a cloud.

I took a breath and ran as fast as I could down our path, and round the corner of the street. Gran only lived through the wall from us, but her front door was right on the other side of her house. It seemed like a long way in the dark.

At her door, I felt something furry scoot around my legs.

'Oh!' I squeaked.

But it was only Puddy.

'Hey, you spooked me! Have you come to see your house? Come on, then.'

I turned the key and pushed open the door.

'Puddy?' I whispered, looking around my feet. But he'd vanished, so I left the front door ajar behind me, and stepped into the hall. Ahh, that nice, washing-powder smell of Gran's house . . .

And it was lovely and warm inside too. I touched the radiator. Someone had put the heating on . . . ?

I turned and squinted into the lounge . . .

And there he was.

Dad.

Right there in front of me, sprawled out on Gran's sofa.

Still in his red slippers.

The curtains weren't drawn and the street light was shining right on him. He was fast asleep under Gran's watching-telly blanket, his mouth open in a quiet snore.

So I *was* right! This WAS where he'd been coming whenever he stayed out late – Gran's empty house. Why hadn't I thought of that before?

And so he *didn't* have a new girl— Oh, BIG phew.

Dad hadn't woken up when I'd come in, so I padded over to him. He was bare-chested under the cover, with both his big arms thrown above his head. I suddenly wanted to giggle. He looked like a giant, chubby baby wrapped in a white, fluffy blankie.

And next to him was a half-eaten piece of Gran's peanut shortbread, and an open tin of condensed milk with a spoon in it.

Sweet milk and a biccie. What a great big baby!

Oh, Dad . . . why did he have to make out he was such a tough man? Really he was a softie on the quiet.

He grunted and wriggled in his sleep so the blanket flopped off him.

I turned away, not wanting to look at his hairy dad body. But not before I'd seen his tattoo on his chest.

I hadn't seen it for ages.

It was a big heart with *Donna* written across it . . . He'd got it when he married Mum. When he used to love her.

Tears prickled my eyes.

A long-time-ago *when* . . .

I covered him with the blanket again, and sat down on the floor next to the sofa.

He woke up then.

'It's OK, Dad,' I whispered. 'It's just me, Courts.' I reached for his hand.

'Courts?' he murmured. 'Oh, I thought you were Mum for a minute there . . .'

Mum? Oh, he means *his* mum . . . Gran.

'Gran's not here, Dad,' I said gently, kissing his hand.

'No, Spud,' he whispered. 'I guess I was just wishing she was.'

It kind of set me off. My tears came again. Really, all I seemed to do was cry!

'Oh, Dad,' I gulped, covering my face with my hands. 'I'm-m scared . . .'

'Scared? What you scared about?' His voice was sleepy and soft.

'EVERYTHING! I'm-m-m-m scare-d-d that . . .' I tried to calm myself so I could speak. 'I'm scared that you'll leave. When you didn't come home again tonight, I got so worried that you and Mum w-w-will split up . . . I even thought you had a girlfriend!'

There, I'd said it.

Then I really sobbed.

He stroked my head with a heavy hand as I cried.

'And I'm so very sorry,' he whispered. 'I thought you'd be fast asleep. I didn't really think you'd notice I wasn't there.'

What?! *As if* . . .

'And I can promise you there's NO girlfriend!' He puffed air out of his cheeks as if the thought exhausted him. 'BUT obviously it IS hard between me and your mother right now . . .'

He paused and looked down at his wedding ring, twirling it round and round his finger. I could tell he was struggling for words. 'We really need to try and sort some stuff out, don't we?' he said with a sigh.

I nodded again, but my tummy had tensed into a hard rock.

Try and sort it out? No! I'd wanted him to say I was being silly and *of course* they weren't going to split up.

I tugged at my bottom lip, twisting it.

'But what does that actually *mean* – "*try*"?' I whispered.

He sighed again, and rolled over, looking right at me in the half-dark.

'Me and your mother have some serious talking to do. But . . .' He sat up and gently stroked my cheek with his finger. 'Look, whatever happens, you'll always be my Spud – forever – and I'll always be your daddy.'

I jumped on his lap then, and hugged his neck like I used to when I was his very little Spud. He hugged me back super-tight.

I leant heavily against him while he fiddled with my hair.

'I love you. And that dopey brother of yours,' he said under his breath. 'Don't forget that.'

I nodded into his prickly neck, tears still blurring my eyes.

'But what about *Mum?*' I said in the tiniest whisper, turning my head so I could see his face.

His eyebrows flicked up, startled.

He scratched his chest for a while, like he was thinking. Or was he actually touching his heart tattoo?

'Yes . . . and her,' he sighed. 'For my sins!'

My heart perked up then. Just a little bit . . .

But now I'd got him listening, I had to tell him about my other worry.

My biggest one.

'And, Dad . . . I'm-m . . . scared that Gran . . .'

I whispered, 'that she'll d—' I couldn't even say the word.

He hugged me tighter.

He didn't say anything for ages. Then he gave an odd gulp, and rubbed his tummy.

'Your gran's a toughie, so we just have to keep believing that she'll pull through the operation.' But he mumbled it so quietly I could only just hear him.

'Operation? What? . . . when?'

'Not sure yet. She needs to get well enough for it.' He coughed and his voice sort of broke. 'There's really nothing else we can do but cross our fingers.'

He hung his head. I thought he was going to burst into tears, but instead his face just went heavy and blank. In the light coming in from the street, he looked more wrinkled up and old than I'd ever seen him.

Oh no, poor Dad.

I wished I could still believe that my dreams could magic everything nice for him. Magic Gran better. But now I wasn't so sure about anything.

Still, I was desperate to see Gran. I was fed up with being banned. And I reckoned it might be a good moment to ask . . .

'Please can I visit Gran, Dad?' I said, squirming up a bit so my cheek was against his. 'It's too hard not seeing her.'

He hesitated.

'I know, Spuddley . . .' He grabbed a pack of tissues from the side.

FLOWERY girlie tissues. Aha, so they were *Gran's*!

He blew his nose for ages. 'It's just that after yesterday, she's got poorlier again, and it's not at all nice seeing her attached to machines and that – just lying there. I think it's better if we wait a bit longer.'

No! I had to go! And if Gran was getting worse, it was even more important . . .

I opened my mouth to argue, but something caught my eye. Something moving by the front door that was still a tiny bit ajar.

Pudds?

No?

It was light-coloured. Small . . .

I dragged my sleeve across my eyes.

OMG, it was Henners!

He scuttled forward and sat on the doormat, shining pure white like some kind of furry little angel in the moonlight.

Glowing.

LIKE IN MY DREAM!

Absolutely, 100% *exactly* like my dream!

It had taken its blinking time, but the magic was back! It truly was. And it had *worked* on Henners.

Which meant it WAS real after all.

Poo to you, Tin Man!

'Dad, look,' I said, pointing at Henners with a shaky arm.

Dad looked . . . and the most enormous grin spread over his face.

I shuffled off his lap and Dad put a nobble of peanut shortbread on his knee. Then Henners trotted over all casual-like, jumped up, and took it in his paws. He sat back and nibbled it politely, gazing at Dad the whole time.

'You cheeky little *wotsit*!' said Dad, shaking his head.

For some reason, that was just really, really funny. And, even though we were both still half crying, we laughed and laughed and laughed.

Chapter Thirty

Me and Dad walked home. The moon was out
from behind the clouds now, sitting fat and bright
in the sky and shimmering silver in all the puddles.
It made the world feel a bit magic.

Ha, magic – wahooooo! I grinned to myself,
and nearly started skipping.

Dad was holding Henners in one hand, and
I held his other one, even though we were only
going a few steps. Down Gran's path, round the
corner, and up our path.

It was so quiet that our footsteps and even

our breathing sounded loud.

'Did you hear that owl?' whispered Dad, stopping with the key in our lock.

I shook my head. I'd been too busy thinking about something . . .

We put Henners to bed. Then Dad sent me up to bed too, with a kiss on the top of my head, saying he would kip on our sofa so he didn't wake Mum.

I snuggled up in my bed. It was so, so late, but I didn't feel sleepy at all. My brain was spinning. Going over and over my idea.

My new, BIG plan.

Mum and Dad weren't going to take me to the hospital – not any time soon, anyway. And now the magic was BACK and WORKING and REAL, there was only one thing for it – I'd have to go by myself.

To try and cure Gran with a worry-magic dream.

I just HAD to. Before her op. Before she got worse . . .

And I wasn't going to tell anyone. Not anyone. Then no one could stop me.

Secret mission!

But the thought was making my insides do bellyflops. And loads of worries were swirling around in my head. What if I got lost on the way? The hospital was so BIG and had so many buildings. What if Gran was too ill to even see me?

It was scary, but I was going to make myself get brave and do it.

And I was going first thing the next morning.

We had an Inset day, so there was no school . . . so no excuse. And I already knew the name of the ward Gran was in.

Chancton Ward.

Dad had written it on the notepad by the hall phone, next to the ward phone number. Along with lots of blue biro doodle pictures of Henners.

Somehow I slept.

But I woke up early and got up straight away.

It was now or never.

I pulled on any old clothes off my chair, stuffed Gran's letter into my pocket, and crept out onto the landing. No Mum, but I could hear Kyle in the bathroom. Maybe he was up early to go for a run. I'd have to hurry, so he didn't ask any awkward questions.

I skulked downstairs, gritting my teeth at every creak. I'd be in big trouble if Mum and Dad knew my plan . . .

Dad was still on the sofa, lying on his tummy, one leg fallen off onto the floor, his slippers still on. He had such a funny, tumbled-up toddler way of sleeping.

Poor Dad. He was so worried about Gran too. His mummy.

But it was OK because I was going to help . . .

I flew around the kitchen on fast-forward, gulping down some banana milk with one hand and scribbling a note with the other: '*Gone swimming. Back later. Love Cxx*'

I slipped out of the front door, glancing up the stairs one more time. No Kyle yet. Good.

I scurried away in the opposite direction to the pool, looking over my shoulder all the time, my heart jumping in my chest. It felt so naughty to pretend, and not do as I was told. But I had to do it. Gran needed my worry magic.

I just hoped I could find her . . .

It started spitting, and then properly tipping down. So I pulled up my hood and ploughed through the rain. Along the high street . . . down some quiet streets, and past a rush-hour traffic jam on the main road.

I got to the hospital car park. The hospital signs looked like the old-fashioned town signs they have in Dick Whittington pantos. One post with lots of arrows pointing in different directions.

MAIN RECEPTION. That would be a start.

I followed the arrow, and took a path through a maze of buildings until I found some huge, swishing doors.

It was busy inside. Nurses in a hurry, people being pushed in wheelchairs. I walked slowly now, past the cafe and shop, staring up at all the different ward names.

CHANCTON ICU.

Was that right?

Dad's note by the phone had said 'Chancton Ward', not ICU, but maybe that was it?

Floor 5.

I went up in the lift. I was worried that someone might think I'd escaped from the children's ward and take me back there, but it was so packed that no one seemed to notice I was by myself.

Another glassy, cold corridor, and then double doors, which said Chancton I.C. Unit across the top.

A young nurse with pink lipstick sat behind a desk. She smiled at me.

'Erm . . . I'm looking for Chancton Ward,' I said. My face was burning up and I was trying not to look guilty.

'You found us,' she said. 'Do you know someone in here?'

'Yes, my gran . . . Pat Ramson.'

'Oh yes, our lovely Pat. But I'm so sorry – it's not visiting time for a couple of hours, and we have to be strict about it, so our patients can get some rest.' Then she sort of frowned. 'And I wouldn't want you to go in alone, love. Are you here by yourself?'

I started to nod, and then stopped myself. 'No . . . my mum . . . she's in the . . . er . . . loo,' I lied, and looked at my feet as even my ears went hot. Such bad lying. I was just rubbish at it.

And what should I do now? She wasn't going to let me in . . . I'd come all this way for nothing.

But I HAD to try and see Gran!

'Is my gran in there?' I said, pointing to a room on the left with a long window. 'Can I just peep at her? Just a teensy peep . . . please.'

The nurse hesitated. 'Well . . . OK . . . but really just for a second.'

She led me to the open door of the ward and pointed in. It was full of people in beds – all with tubes and machines and stuff.

'There's Pat – she's sleeping –' the nurse began. Then the phone started ringing, so she squeezed my shoulder and went back to her desk.

I couldn't even see Gran at first, and then I did.

She was two beds along, but half behind a curtain. Her eyes were closed and she was flopped out on her bed, wearing a nightie and some funny, stretchy, white hospital tights.

I could see tubes coming out of her arm and chest, attached to machines.

My heart sped up. She looked SO little and thin. Not really like Gran at all.

My tummy started butterflying. I couldn't swallow.

Poor Gran – she really looked worse than I thought. It was horrible. How would she ever get better?

I took some long breaths and put my palm on the window to steady myself. Whoa – wobbly . . .

And then I realised what was happening. The worry magic was on its way.

It actually was!

The world was turning and my legs were like mush.

I let it take me.

I put my back against the cold wall, and slid down it onto the floor.

Chapter Thirty-one

The dream was the slowest and clearest ever.
And it was more like a film this time, except I
was looking out of my own eyes.

I was by Gran's bed. I touched her hand,
and she looked up and gave me a huge smile.
Then she pulled back her covers, swung out
of bed, tugging out all her tubes – it didn't
even seem to hurt her. Then she took her pink
checked coat and her best butterfly scarf out
of her cupboard, and put them on ready to
go home . . .

Then a phone rang. LOUD. I startled out of my dream and pinged open my eyes.

The nurse!

No, it was okay – she was talking on the phone again. She hadn't even noticed me on the floor.

I jumped to my feet quickly.

OMG. That dream was more than awesome. Gran had even put on her coat and scarf ready to leave. It *had* to have come true! I'd worried SO much about Gran that I'd surely made some very STRONG worry magic. But now I needed to get over to Gran so it could all happen . . .

The lipsticky nurse was still talking at her desk, her back turned.

So, double-quick, I scampered into the ward.

I was at Gran's bedside in a second.

Oh, it was happening just right! Just like I'd dreamt it.'

'Gran?' I squeaked, a big lump rising in my throat.

'It's OK, sweetheart. I'm just a bit weedy,' she wheezed in a tiny, cracked voice.

But she was more than weedy. I could see that. She was very ill.

I rocked on my feet.

The magic hadn't worked!

But why not? There was no reason this time. I'd worried well, and the dream had been perfect.

I let out the biggest sob.

I kind of staggered, and fell onto my knees next to the bed, burying my head in her blankets.

'Oh, Gran! I can't make you better, can I . . .'

The desk nurse came rushing in just then, pulling at my arm, telling me to mind Gran's tubes, saying loads of stuff, but I wasn't listening at all.

I just stayed there, hugging Gran tighter as sob after sob shuddered through me.

Gran was patting my head and making the soft, soothing humming she used to make if we got hurt when we were little.

I didn't want to let go of her – not ever, ever.

Chapter Thirty-two

The nurse was trying to be nice about it, but she wasn't one bit happy.

'I can see you're upset. But you really must come back at visiting time,' she said, crisply. 'Please let me help you find your mother now.'

Gran patted my head.

'Where's Mum, darling?' she whispered, huskily. 'Best find her and come back later, eh, baby girl?'

'But Mum and Dad won't LET me,' I wailed, still clinging to her. 'I've been asking and asking to come! And I've got *loads* to tell you . . . I've been so, so worried.'

I yanked my letter out of my pocket. 'I even wrote you a letter about it!'

The nurse said something about the matron, but I didn't take any notice of her. Then I heard her turn and leave.

I tore open the envelope and put my letter in Gran's hand. 'Can you see? There's some Puddy fur on it.' But she couldn't really see properly without lifting her head, and she didn't have her glasses on. So I took her finger and stroked it on the fur that was sticking out from the Sellotape.

'Puddy misses you too much, Gran,' I gulped. 'He can't bear it without you.'

Gran looked up at me sadly, brought my hand to her face and kissed it. 'He can manage much better than he thinks, you know,' she said, softly.

I didn't really know what Gran meant, so I turned the letter over.

'And look – on the bac-k-k,' I stuttered, 'I wrote a whole list of worry-wig worries for you. I even guessed some of the flavours, but they might not be right.'

She smiled gently then.

'What a good idea to write them down!' she said, in a weak voice. 'But even better, next to each worrying thing, you could write one *good* thing that might happen too . . . Can you do that? Show me it next time?'

'OK, Gran . . . I'll try,' I whispered. Even though I couldn't think of any good things . . . not any.

I laid my head on her arm again, being careful not to bang any of her tubes. Her blankets didn't smell like Gran – they smelt of nothing, like dust.

Out of the corner of my eye, I could see the nurse outside the ward window, talking to a much older nurse in a different uniform, pointing over and frowning – I knew she was telling on me. Then they both started marching towards the door, looking like they weren't going to be put off this time.

'They're coming to get me now, Gran,' I said, sitting up. 'But don't worry – I'll come again soon! Even if Mum and Dad won't bring me. I'll just climb the wall like . . . er . . . Puddy! He can come too!'

I cuddled her one last time, and then just ran. Past the nurses and out of the ward, throwing myself against the heavy doors, and sprinting down the cold, glassy corridor. By the time I got to the lifts, I was crying so much that I couldn't even see where I was going.

The worry magic hadn't worked on Gran, and I had no idea why not . . .

But what I did know was that I couldn't save her – not with magic, nor without it.

Dad was right – there was nothing we could do but hope.

Except Gran looked so poorly . . . so *hopeless* . . .

The lifts were all closed. I stabbed all the buttons loads of times, but still none of them came.

For ages.

Then finally a lift door opened.

And there was Kyle.

Chapter Thirty-three

'You left your yellow swimming bag behind, so I knew you hadn't gone to the pool,' Kyle said, matter-of-factly, holding the lift with his foot. 'And I somehow guessed you were coming here. But then it took me ages to find the right ward.'

I nodded. My lips trembled, and then I burst.

'The magic didn't w-w-ork,' I spluttered through my sobs. 'I came to worry Gran better. And I had a dream, but she's stayed poorly. And then I got thrown out.'

Kyle didn't say anything. He didn't even roll his eyes. He just pulled me into the lift. On the ground floor, he took me by the shoulders and guided me, along the hospital corridors, through all the people and out of the exit. I was crying so much my teeth were chattering. When we got outside, he turned his back to me and stretched out his arms behind him.

'Jump on,' he said, quietly.

So I did. And he carried me piggy-back all the way home, through the pelting rain. He took a winding way home, down emptier streets, so we didn't see anyone. I think he was doing that for me, but I didn't care who saw us. I just pulled up my hood, hid my face in the back of his neck and cried.

He didn't say anything and he didn't stop – except to shrug me higher up his back – even though I must have weighed a total ton.

When we got back, he dropped me down on our doorstep. He was bright red and puffing like mad.

'Thank you,' I whispered, wiping my face on my coat.

He just nodded.

But then when we stepped into the porch, we both heard it.

Mum and Dad inside. Screaming and shouting *again*. Surely Dad should be at work by now?

We froze and looked each other.

'I bought the van for MY new business,' Mum was yelling. 'You can't just nick it for yours.'

'I don't see why I can't use it as well,' Dad growled back. 'I've got to transport my tools and mower somehow. And I paid for it too.'

OMG, Mum must've shown Dad the ice-cream van. And now they were fighting over it. Just like I'd worried they would when I'd got her to hide it at the sanctuary.

Except I'd never guessed they'd argue because they both WANTED it.

I sighed. However well I worried, I'd never be able to think of everything that might go wrong, would I? Not without a fairy crystal ball. It was pointless too. The magic only lasted ten minutes, and then they fought again.

And it hadn't even worked on the most important thing . . . Gran.

I looked at Kyle, expecting him to tell me to keep out of it, like he usually did. But he didn't say anything. He just bent down and started untying his trainers, so I couldn't see his face.

Not that he needed to say anything to me. I was going to leave well alone this time. I'd actually had it with trying to fix them. I just felt zombie-tired – like I could sleep for a billion, trillion years.

But we still needed to get past them into the house. I wondered if we should put our shoes back on, and nip round to the back door

I tugged at Kyle's sleeve to say that, but he wouldn't look at me. He was staring straight ahead at the door, listening to Mum and Dad go on and on. His cheeks were even redder under his freckles now, and his hands were balled up. Suddenly his nose wrinkled, and then without a word, he rammed the door open with his foot and stamped into the lounge. I followed in behind, gawping.

'MUM, DAD!' His voice filled the room. 'JUST STOP IT!'

Mum and Dad both turned around with shocked faces, and shut up instantly. No one had ever heard Kyle shout like that before. It didn't even sound like his voice.

This was so unlike keep-your-head-down, Tin-Man Kyle that we all simply stared at him like he'd just walked through a wall or something.

'YOU JUST FIGHT ALL THE TIME,' he roared. 'SO WHY DON'T YOU JUST SPLIT UP AND GIVE US ALL SOME PEACE? WHY DON'T YOU THINK ABOUT *US* FOR A CHANGE?'

He was shaking – juddering from head to foot. I was scared he might even fall over, so I stepped forward and put my arm round him to hold him up.

'I'm so sorry –' whispered Mum in a cracked voice. 'I'm so sorry, Kylsie . . .'

'Yes, son . . .' began Dad, putting his hand out to Kyle. 'I'm –'

But Kyle slapped his hand away and bounded up the stairs two at a time.

I gave Mum and Dad both a daggers look and ran up the stairs after Kyle.

Chapter Thirty-four

Kyle's bedroom door was shut.

I knocked gently, went in and closed the door behind me. *Keep out, parents.*

Kyle was right under his Man U duvet – all I could see were some hamstery tufts of hair sticking out on his pillow.

'It's just me,' I whispered. 'Can I come in?'

He nodded his head, snuffling.

I clambered onto the end of his bed, and sat with my back against the wall, and my feet under his duvet.

We were quiet for a while, apart from the odd sniffle from Kyle.

'That was so cool,' I said. 'You really TOLD them.'

'Yeah, like it's going to make any difference!' said Kyle, propping himself up on one elbow. He didn't have his glasses on, his hair was all rumpled, and his face was still pink and damp. It made him look sort of younger.

'But you made them stop . . . and listen!' I said.

'Huh,' he said. 'Well, they only made nice, because they didn't want to upset you.'

'No . . . not me . . . YOU!' I said.

He shrugged, and scrubbed his eyes with his fists. It was like he really thought they only cared about ME.

'They love us *both*, you know,' I whispered. 'Silly.'

He shrugged again and puffed out a big breath.

'Well, I guess they do,' he sighed. 'Your magic wouldn't work if they didn't.' And he gave me a little smile.

I couldn't believe my ears.

'Ah! Since when d'you believe in magic, Tin Man?'

'I dunno. Just that kind, maybe.'

'That kind?'

'You know . . .' He glanced away, a bit coy. 'Love and all that.'

He flicked my knee. 'But don't tell anyone, Hermione.'

He said it kindly, so I didn't scowl.

I leant my head back, tracing the strands of cobweb that looped across Kyle's ceiling, back and forth with my eyes.

'But what if they actually DO split up?' I said, under my breath, half to myself.

'It'll be bleak,' said Kyle from his pillow. 'But we'd cope.'

'Even without Gran?' I said. 'Oh, Kyle, she looks so bad. What if she never comes home again?'

Kyle didn't answer.

There was a long pause – tears were trickling slowly down my throat and back off my cheeks into my ears. And then suddenly Kyle spun over onto his tummy and buried his face in his pillow.

He was crying.

It took me completely by surprise. Kyle was like Dad in that way – he never cried. That had always been my job.

I crawled up his bed and lay along next to him, patting him awkwardly while he shook.

'We just have to hope and *hope* that the operation works and Gran gets better,' I said, my tears plopping onto his duvet. 'And we'll go and see her loads – every day! – we'll MAKE Mum and Dad take us.'

He nodded into his pillow while I rubbed his back. It was like all of a sudden I was older and he was very little.

Then we didn't speak for ages.

'And by the way, I'm going to come and watch you play footie,' I whispered, resting my chin on his back. '*Even* if Dad doesn't.'

He just stuck his hand out of the covers, grabbed my hand and squeezed it.

Chapter Thirty-five

I slid out to the loo.

But Mum was on the landing when I opened the door, folding clean towels into the airing cupboard.

'Oh, there you are, Courts, darling.' She went pink, and stuffed a towel unfolded onto the shelf. 'Is Kyle OK?'

I just looked at my feet, and didn't answer.

She came over and hugged me, and I let her.

'I wanted to tell you and Kyle something,' she said into my hair. 'Me and Dad realise things have got completely out of hand, so we've agreed to go to Relate. You know, like counselling . . .'

Counselling. What was that, then?

Mum had taken my shoulders, and was holding me away from her so she could look at me. I could tell she was going to get all lovey-dovey, but then the doorbell rang.

'Oh,' said Mum, glancing towards the stairs. 'That might be Lois for you – she came earlier, when you were out. She said she'd pop back.'

Lois?

I hopped down into the hall.

Lois was in the porch. Her hair and coat were soaking.

'Raining.' She grinned and shook some raindrops at me. 'Let me in, then.'

She stepped into the hall.

'You didn't reply to my text! And I really want you to come swimming with me!' She prodded my tummy with her finger.

'What . . . with you and *Bex*?' I said, rolling my eyes a bit.

'No, you plank!' said Lois. 'I don't want to be

mean, but it really wasn't any fun going with her. She's just *no good* at swimming.' She lowered her voice as if Bex might overhear. 'She took ages to get in, and didn't even want to get her hair wet. And when I splashed her by accident, she just sort of screamed and sank!'

I couldn't help sniggering at that. It was too funny.

Then suddenly I felt a bit sheepish. Like I'd made a big fuss over nothing.

I gave her a wide grin.

'Look, I ditched you on your birthday, so I owe you cake and a swim . . . so maybe we could go right now, this minute?' I said, tugging on her soggy plait like a bell rope. 'Or did you already swim in some puddles?'

'Oh, I was hoping you'd say that,' she cried. 'I've got my cossie on under my clothes! And my lemon-jelly bag in your porch. Let's DO it!'

She came upstairs with me to get my cossie and a towel.

As we passed Mum and Dad's room, I could hear them both in there arguing, but in hushed voices like they didn't want us to hear.

Again . . .

I couldn't wait to be in that water with Lois.

Just away from here.

I got my towel and popped my head into Kyle's room to see if he was OK.

'I'm off swimming,' I said. He was sitting at his desk, plugged into a computer game. He looked calmer now. Back like himself again.

'Oh, OK . . . and hi, Lo,' he called, when he saw her head bobbing behind me.

'Hi!' she said, waving.

We both stepped into his room for a second.

'And can you tell Mum and Dad I've gone, because – guess what? – they're having a fight in their room. They're trying to shout quietly, but it's not working.'

Kyle shook his head.

'Obviously they are.'

'But, hey, do you know what Mum said? She said they're going to Relate counselling or something.'

Kyle's eyes went wide then. He already seemed to know what Relate was.

'But what *is* that exactly?' I asked.

'It's like . . . they'll go and talk to someone about their problems,' Kyle said.

I nodded. That had to be good, didn't it? It was something, at least.

Lois was just standing there, looking back and forth between us.

'I'll explain later,' I said to her, and she nodded.

I didn't mind at all if she knew about the big Mum-and-Dad trouble . . . In fact it might be good to talk to her about it. She *was* my best friend after all.

'Yeah, well . . .' Kyle muttered, 'Good luck to the counsellor, that's all I can say. She's gonna need a blinking magic wand to fix those two.'

Then he realised what he'd said and laughed. And I laughed too.

I liked having an in-joke with him.

'Uh?' said Lois. 'What's so funny?'

'Nah, it's just Kyle. He loves magic,' I said. 'He can't shut up about it, can you, big bro?' And I went over and hugged Kyle's head, blowing a raspberry into his hair. He sort of let me, grinning.

'See you later!' I said.

As we went downstairs, Lois said,

'Aww, it's so nice you get on with Kyle like that. Max can't really be bothered with me much.'

'Hmmm,' I said. It *was* nice. New but nice.

I remembered then what Gran had said about writing down good things that might happen, as well as my worries.

Maybe I could write – *Getting a bit more friends with Kyle* . . .

Or – *Having Lois back to talk to.*

It had stopped raining out.

I looked at Lois and grinned at her cheekily.

'Last one there has to ask Cavey if she is growing her moustache for Movember!' I cried, starting to run.

And we raced along the road to the pool, pushing each other into puddles and laughing.

Acknowledgements

Big thanks to the ever-astute James Catchpole for all your support and brainy brilliance.

A massive thank-you to the tip-top and utterly marvellous team at HKB – most of all, the lovely Emma Matthewson.

Thanks to Eddie and Esther for being my consultants on school life; and to Gooner for being my muse and furry foot-warmer.

And much love, big hugs and thank-yous to Steve, Poppy and Lola for dealing with all MY worry-worry-worrying.

Dawn McNiff

Dawn was born in a blue house by the sea in Sussex. She now lives in a brown house in Gloucestershire with her two teenage daughters and lots of furry pets. In 2008 she did an MA in Writing for Young People at Bath Spa University, which was 100% fab. In the past, she has worked as a bereavement counsellor, a copywriter, a teaching assistant and a children's bookseller – but her best job has always been being a mummy. Dawn likes dancing to bad 80s songs, going for rainy walks, eating green soup, snoozing by her log-burner, and writing in cafes. (PS: Never challenge Dawn to a water fight cos you'll lose.) Follow Dawn on Twitter: @DawnMcNiff

HOT KEY BOOKS

Thank you for choosing a Hot Key book.

If you want to know more about our authors
and what we publish, you can find us online.

You can start at our website

www.hotkeybooks.com

And you can also find us on:

We hope to see you soon!